To Natal
Hope yo
hunky ghost!

Ghostly Persuasion
An Emerald Isle Enchantment Novel

By

Dena Garson

Space Coast 22
Dena
Garson

Ghostly Persuasion
Copyright © 2016 Dena Garson
Edited by Faith Van Horne
Previously released by Ellora's Cave on July 12, 2013

Cover art by Cover Couture (http://www.bookcovercouture.com)
Photo Copyright: Kanuman / Shutterstock
Photo Copyright: alessandro guerriero / Shutterstock
Photo Copyright: Rob Stark / Shutterstock

ISBN: 978-1-945075-09-4 (print)

DEDICATION

For my boys – if you can dream it you can do.

ACKNOWLEDGMENTS

The authors I worked with to create the world of the Emerald Isle Fantasies are a great bunch of ladies! It was my first collaboration effort and I value the experience and the friendships that came out of it. Virginia Cavanaugh, Jennifer LaRose, Katalina Leon, Louisa Masters, Rebecca Royce, and Rea Thomas you are all fabulous!

.

1

"**CALL** me when you get to Belfast. I don't care if it is the middle of the night," Jenny said as she hugged her best friend Katie tightly.

"I will." Katie returned the embrace. "I promise."

"And when you get to the hotel too. If it's half as nice as the pictures we saw on their website, you'll be spoiled before you get home."

"We'll see," Katie said with a grin.

"I gave the attendant your bags," Paul, Jenny's new husband, said as he joined them. "Here's your baggage claim ticket." He handed the ticket to Katie then slipped one arm around Jenny's waist.

"Thanks, Paul."

"Hey, you be careful over there, okay?" he said, sounding very much like a big brother.

"I will." She gave Jenny another quick hug. "I'm not going to run up a phone bill by calling you every day, but I will email or text. Okay?"

"Okay."

"Good luck with the house-hunting while I'm gone. And seriously, don't worry about trying to rush out and find something right away. We can work something out when I get back."

"All right. I love you, sis."

Jenny and Katie had been best friends since the third grade. They weren't related by blood but they considered each other sisters of the heart.

"I love you too." Katie gave Paul one last smile, happy that Jenny had found someone to love who loved her just as much in return, then headed to the airline's check-in desk.

"Let me know if you find out what Irishmen wear under their kilts!" Jenny shouted just as Katie got in line at the desk.

Katie rolled her eyes and waved in Jenny's direction to let her know she'd heard. A barely stifled chuckle nearby told Katie that everyone else in line had too. She loved Jenny dearly but sometimes she wanted to just choke her.

She finished her check-in at the counter and made her way through security. After reading all the requirements for bringing cremated remains, she was surprised she didn't have more trouble. Thank God for the funeral home and their willingness to help her find a travel-friendly container for her mother's ashes. One that could go through the x-ray machine without a problem.

When she arrived at the departure gate, she found a chair out of the way then sat down and dug one of the many paperbacks from her bag. Katie didn't recognize the cover so she flipped it over to read the blurb on the back. The book was a romance about a modern-day woman who had been transported back in time while visiting an ancient castle in Ireland. Of course the heroine fell in love with the Irish warrior whose lap she literally had fallen into.

Katie snorted. Jenny must have slipped the book into her bag when she wasn't looking. The brat. Must be trying to tell her to keep an eye out for hunky Irish heroes while overseas.

Well… The idea did have merit. After all, none of Katie's recent romances had worked out. Maybe a fling with an Irish hunk would be just what she needed before she returned home, looked for a new job and started a new routine. In between all the castles, sheep farms and rolling hillsides that she wanted to see, that is.

A man dressed in a pinstriped suit and wing tip shoes, leaning over the shoulder of a rather well-endowed woman, interrupted her daydreaming. His semi-transparent form hinted that he no longer belonged in the mortal world. She rolled her eyes when she saw he wasn't reading the woman's magazine, just enjoying the view down her low-cut blouse. Even in death, men were drawn to boobs.

She struggled to keep her eyes on her book instead of on the apparitions she spotted around the terminal. From the different styles of dress, she guessed the airport had been around for a while. She shuddered to think of the number of accidents that occurred in the area to tie so many spirits to this location.

Or were ghosts able to fly on a plane and travel to other places?

An intriguing thought. She'd never taken the time to sit and talk with any ghosts. Only when someone had an urgent need to do so. She'd always spent more time pretending she didn't have the ability to see or hear them.

Before she knew it, the attendant came on the intercom to begin boarding for their flight.

Each of her flights went surprisingly smoothly. Even getting through customs hadn't been as much of an ordeal as she had feared. Thanks to the sleeping pill she took before boarding the plane for the flight into Belfast, Katie dozed for a few hours and felt somewhat rejuvenated when they landed.

The assistant at her mother's law firm who made the travel arrangements provided excellent directions and made finding the car service very easy. She enjoyed being ushered into the back of a limousine more than she should. If her trip started off with a limo ride, she couldn't wait to see the castle-turned-hotel.

The driver introduced himself as Thomas. The short, somewhat pudgy man had a friendly face and a mischievous twinkle in his eye. He reminded her of Michaleen from *The Quiet Man*.

Katie immediately moved to the seat closest to the driver so she could talk with Thomas along the way. He kindly pointed out important landmarks as they passed. He even slowed the car whenever she expressed an interest in something so she could take a longer look.

His stories made the long drive pass faster than Katie expected.

"There's a lot of history in Ireland, miss. I'm sure if there were something you wanted to be seeing, they could arrange for you to find your way there from the castle. That Alanna is a fine one for making sure her guests are satisfied," Thomas said.

"Is Alanna the hotel manager?"

Thomas chuckled. "That and many other things. After finishing at the university, she returned home and worked her way up through the ranks. Said she didn't want special treatment just because she was family. By the time her grandfather passed she could be credited for having doubled the tour business to the area. It was no surprise when she inherited Tullamore from her grandfather. She's been running things since."

"Sounds as if she knows what she's doing."

"Aye. That she does."

The car rattled across an ancient-looking bridge. When they made it to the other side Katie felt a brush of energy ripple across her skin.

"Wha—"

"We're on Tullamore land now, miss."

Katie swiveled her head in both directions, trying to look out the windows on both sides of the car at the same time.

She could see lush forests along one side. On the other, rolling meadows dotted with gray poofs that looked a bit like sheep. Zigzagging over and across the hills were short walls made of stone that made Katie think of small cottages and fairy tales her mother used to tell.

The road turned sharply to the left and part of the castle came into view. Several tower-like sections reached up above the tree line. Off to the right sat an imposing tower that supported the castle's flags.

A mix of emotions rolled through Katie. Her curiosity about her mother's former life amplified her excitement at being in a new place. Those were both dampened by a wave of loneliness at how much she missed her mom.

Thomas turned off the road they had been traveling and passed through a gatehouse onto what Katie guessed was the main estate driveway. The drive ran alongside a river and then made a loop in front of the hotel. The view of the estate took her breath away.

As they rolled down the drive Katie tried to keep her eyes on the structure, rather than the half dozen or more ghostly figures they passed. There were more here than she had ever seen at one time. Some of the ghosts were riding ghostly horses which made it even harder to not stare. She prayed her face wouldn't betray her.

"Here you are, miss." Thomas pulled the car near what looked like the main entrance to the hotel and put the gear shift into park.

Katie gathered her things and rummaged through her purse for a suitable tip as Thomas got out and came around to her side of the car. He had been such good company on the drive and she wanted to thank him properly.

Thomas opened her door then offered his hand to help her out.

When she climbed out and looked up at the castle, her eyes were immediately drawn to the gray stone figures at the top. Griffins, if she remembered her lore correctly. The history and the beauty of the castle both excited and overwhelmed her. From the corner of her eye she saw more than one hazy figure drifting about the castle grounds.

Some inner sense told her that her arrival had captured the attention of more than one person.

"Are you all right, miss?" Thomas asked when she made no move to enter the castle.

Katie shook aside her worry. "Yes, I'm fine. Just overwhelmed by how big the castle is up close."

"Ah. I suppose it is. But you'll be well taken care of here. Don't you worry."

"I'm sure you're right, Thomas." Katie pasted a smile on her face. "So I guess I need to check in somewhere just inside then?"

"If you'll go up the stairs and through those doors, you'll find a long counter. Anyone working there can help you."

Katie opened her mouth to ask about her bags but Thomas beat her to it. "I'll have one of these strapping lads…" He pointed to a couple of tall, thin young men wearing matching uniforms and who were headed in their direction. "Bring your bags in. The front desk will have them delivered to your room."

"Thank you, Thomas. You certainly made the drive out here fun. I loved your stories and hearing the history of the area." She handed him the bills she had pulled from her wallet.

"Thank you, miss. And when you get ready to return to the airport, you ask for me. I'll be happy to come and carry you off."

"I will do that." Katie smiled then turned to head to the main doors.

As if by magic, one of the oversized wooden doors opened when she approached. *Must have one of those sensors like many department stores.* Even though she couldn't hear it, she'd wager the motor had to be oversized in order to manage the weight of such gargantuan doors.

Katie stepped into a large open area. Couches and chairs had been scattered about the room creating multiple seating areas. Rugs had been laid in each of the areas. Most likely to absorb the sound across the dark stone floor. A massive chandelier hung from a large chain attached to the ceiling. She wondered if the fixture had been around when the castle had first been built then fitted for electrical lights later. It fit the décor of the castle perfectly.

When she realized she blocked the doorway as she stood gaping like a tourist, Katie roused herself and headed to the long wooden desk Thomas had mentioned.

"Good afternoon. Checking in?" the young man behind the

desk asked.

"Yes, please," Katie replied as she dropped her bag onto the floor beside her.

"And your name?"

"Katherine Ward."

The young man typed something into his computer. "Ah, yes, Miss Ward. I see you'll be staying with us for three weeks. Is that correct?"

"Yes."

"That's unusual," he mumbled then looked up at Katie with his brows furrowed. "It says your reservation was made more than three years ago?"

Katie nodded and swallowed the lump that automatically formed in her throat anytime she thought of her mother. "Yes, that's probably about right."

"Wow. Okay, let me see which room we have reserved for you."

"I'll take care of Miss Ward, Peter," said a petite woman with bright-red hair as she came through a door in the paneled wall behind the desk. The woman wore a gray pinstriped suit and had a look on her face that brooked no argument.

"Oh yes, of course, ma'am." The young man nodded in almost a short bow then moved to the other end of the long desk and shuffled whatever paperwork he found there.

"Miss Ward, I'm Alanna Burke. I'm the owner of Tullamore Castle." Alanna leaned across the desk and extended her hand.

Katie noticed a white lace handkerchief peeking out of Alanna's sleeve as she took the woman's hand. "It's nice to meet you, Ms. Burke." Alanna certainly didn't have a wimpy grip.

"It's a pleasure to finally meet you, Miss Ward. We've been looking forward to your arrival."

"Oh, well, thank you."

Alanna dropped her voice slightly. "I, and several members of our staff, knew your mother and remember her fondly. I was very sorry to hear of her passing."

"Thank you."

"I understand it was her last wish that her remains be returned to Ireland? Specifically to Tullamore?"

"Yes, that's right."

"I will need to finish looking into a couple of things. If you wouldn't mind waiting until the end of your stay to fulfill the request, I believe we will be in a position to assist you."

"Um. Okay." Katie tucked a stray strand of hair behind her ear. "I guess I can do that."

"Very good." Alanna nodded briskly then looked down at the computer screen. "Now let's see about your room."

She typed something then mumbled, "Yes, I think that will do nicely."

Katie looked around the lobby as she waited for Alanna to finish whatever she needed to do on the computer. Despite all the stone and rough wood, the room had a cozy yet elegant feel. She was even more pleased to not see any ghosts.

Alanna looked up from her typing. "Tug?" she called across the room.

A tall, lanky, teenaged boy hurried to the desk. "Yes, Ms. Burke?"

"Would you please make sure Miss Ward's luggage is taken to suite 201?"

"Two hundred and one? But isn't that—"

Alanna silenced Tug with a look.

"Yes, ma'am." Tug hurried away to do as she had asked.

"Is there a problem with the room?" Katie asked.

"Not at all." Alanna picked up the pages she had just printed and put them on the desk in front of Katie along with a pen.

Katie scanned the document. It was a standard room reservation except it had a balance due of zero. "Mom even paid for the room in advance?"

"Payment has been prearranged."

"I see." Alanna's answer didn't make Katie comfortable but she didn't know what had transpired between her mother, the lawyers and any of the staff at Tullamore. Knowing it would be pointless to argue, she signed the check-in slip and slid the papers back across the desk to Alanna.

"Very good. Here is your copy." She folded the paper into thirds and handed it to Katie. "Now let me show you to your room."

"You don't have to do that. I'm sure I can find my way."

"Don't be ridiculous. Of course I'm going to show you to your room." Alanna looked offended that Katie had thought otherwise.

Alanna put away the documents and produced two room-access

key cards. She made her way around the end of the long counter. "If you'll follow me, please?"

Katie strongly suspected that had been more of a command than a request. Still, she grabbed her bag and followed Alanna to the elevator.

"There are two modern lifts in the hotel. There is also a much older model in the family wing if you're interested in a bit of history. Most of our guests avoid using it however. You'll also find stairs here to your right." She indicated a carpeted staircase that curved around the elevator shaft.

"Tullamore has a lot of history," Alanna continued as she pressed the button to call the elevator. "As a guest at the hotel, you'll have full access to the gardens and grounds. There is a brochure in your room that will describe many of the activities in and around the castle. You can also call the front desk if you have any questions or need to locate anything."

The elevator doors opened, saving Katie from having to reply. She followed Alanna into the elevator then noticed the second floor lit on the control panel. Had she known they were only going up one flight she would have suggested they take the stairs. Without luggage it would have been an easy climb. Speaking of bags, she hoped it wouldn't take long for them to deliver hers.

"Your luggage will have been delivered to your room already."

The elevator came to a stop and the doors opened while Katie gaped at Alanna. It took an effort to shake off the notion that Alanna had read her mind. She hurried out of the elevator to follow her to the appropriate room.

Katie found Alanna a few doors down the hallway sliding the keycard through a lock. Alanna opened the door then held it so Katie could pass ahead of her.

Katie had assumed she would be given a regular hotel room. The opulent furnishings and size of the suite she had been given left her astounded. "Wow."

Alanna breezed in behind Katie and headed to the windows on the far side. She pulled the curtains aside and let in what was left of the sun.

If there were any problems with the suite Katie didn't see them. Thankfully that included ghosts.

"You'll be able to observe the main gardens from here," Alanna said. "And, as I'm sure you noticed, you'll have ready access to the lobby."

"That will be nice," Katie murmured, still enthralled by her surroundings. She wondered if it had been part of the original castle or a later addition.

Alanna crossed the room to an open doorway. "I'm afraid renovations have not been completed in this suite. While the bathroom has been completely redone," she flicked on the lights, "the bedroom area has not."

"But it's lovely as it is."

"Thank you. We have been preserving as much of the original structure as possible with our renovations but we also want to ensure our guests' comfort. Many of our rooms now have thermostat-controlled fireplaces that allow our guests to better regulate the room temperature. Wiring is also being upgraded to incorporate current technology for all the gadgets everyone carries these days."

"I imagine I'll be perfectly comfortable in here, even without those things."

"I certainly hope so. We do try to exceed our guests' expectations."

Katie, curious to see what the bathroom looked like, crossed the room to the doorway.

"Oh my." Sand-colored tile covered the floor, walls, and ceiling. The sinks were white porcelain and the silver fixtures gleamed as if they had just been polished. *This must be what bathrooms in heaven look like.*

"I believe you will find everything you need in either the nooks on either side of the mirror or the linen closet at the end of the counter." Alanna pointed to a small door at the far end of the bathroom.

"I'm sure," Katie mumbled, still dumbstruck. The enormous tub in the center of the room held her attention.

"Many of our guests have reported that a long soak in a hot bath using the lavender bath salts helped them unwind after their flights."

"That sounds absolutely wonderful."

"I will leave you to it then." Alanna headed to the suite entrance then paused. "Your bags have been left next to the bed and your room access cards are on the table next to the window. Please call the front desk if there's anything you need."

Katie dragged her gaze away from the tub to respond. "Thank you. I will."

Alanna nodded then slipped out, quietly shutting the door behind her.

Katie took one more look at the tub. *Oh yeah. That was definitely getting used tonight.*

2

"OH my God, Jenny. You should see this place," Katie exclaimed into the phone.

"Is it as wonderful as their website showed?"

"Even better." Katie spun herself around in the middle of her suite. The furnishings and the ambience and the fact that she was in a twelfth- century castle still held her in awe. "They must have done a lot of work to keep this place in such good shape."

"I'll bet. You do have indoor plumbing then, huh?" Jenny teased.

"It looks like I have my own spa in here," Katie said as she paraded back into the marble-lined bathroom for the fifth time. "The bathtub could hold three of me and the shower has one of those fancy waterfall fixtures. Funny thing is, despite it being completely covered with stone or tile, it's not cold. I think the floor is heated somehow."

"Oooo… Send me a picture so I can be even more jealous."

"I hate it that Mom spent so much money. There is no way this was a cheap trip."

"Your mom loved you, Katie. Just think of it as her way of spoiling you one last time."

Katie sighed into the phone. "I really miss her."

"I know you do. So do I."

Katie sniffed back the tears she felt coming and forced herself to focus on how wonderful her room was. "All right, I better go. I need to see if I can get some sleep so I can adjust to this time zone. And I don't want to run up a huge phone bill."

"Okay. I'm glad you made it safely." Jenny yawned, making Katie regret waking her up so early.

"I'll let you know what I'm doing throughout the week."

"Okay, sis. You have fun over there. And keep an eye out for available, hunky Irishmen."

Katie rolled her eyes. "Yeah, okay. I'll be sure I do that."

"Send me pictures when you do," Jenny said with another yawn.

"Uh huh. Sorry to wake you. I'll talk to you later."

Katie clicked off her cell phone and dropped it into her jeans pocket. She unpacked about half of her clothes as she dug around looking for clean underwear and a t-shirt to sleep in. Her body felt tired but she wasn't sleepy and the lure of the oversized bathtub was more than she could resist.

She turned on the water, found a temperature to suit her then added some of the bath salts that were sitting on the ledge over the tub. The smell of fresh lavender floated up with the steam rising from the water.

If that didn't help her relax, nothing would.

She dropped her dirty clothes onto the floor then kicked them into the corner, out of the way. She made a mental note to find her laundry bag later. Just before stepping into the decadent-smelling water and steam, she remembered to grab an extra towel off the rack at the end of the counter.

When she sank into the steamy bath she sighed with pleasure.

Now this she could get used to quickly.

Katie allowed her thoughts to drift and float where they wanted. Some of them were based in reality, like what she would need to do about finding a roommate when she returned home. The others were nowhere near being real. Her mind strayed to the idea that a hunky Irishman showed up in her room and offered to rub away all her aches and pains. He, of course, would know exactly where to touch her and would want nothing more than to spend all day and night pleasuring her.

Then, after making love to her multiple times, he would declare his undying devotion to her.

She snorted to herself. *Yeah right. And maybe monkeys will fly out of my butt too.*

It was a lovely daydream however. Especially the part where she had three orgasms before leaving the bathroom. Twice in the tub and once while bent over the vanity counter. Her fantasy man was extremely talented.

Katie sighed as she stepped out of the tub. It was too bad no such man existed outside of Jenny's beloved romance novels.

As she dried off she thought about her last few boyfriends. None of them had created that special spark she felt should have been there. As much as she cared for her last boyfriend Alan, she was glad now that he had panicked and broken up with her right before their college graduation. It hurt at the time but, looking back, it had been the right thing.

She hadn't told Alan about her "gift". That alone should have been a big indicator the relationship wasn't going to work. If she didn't feel comfortable enough confiding that information, something had definitely been missing.

After rubbing some lotion on, she slipped into a clean pair of boyshorts and pulled a t-shirt over her head. With her hair wrapped in a towel, she padded out to the bedroom. As soon as she had a clear view of the four-poster bed she skidded to a stop, stunned by the sight of a strange man lounging against the headboard.

"Excuse me, but what are you doing?" Katie demanded.

The man continued to stare up at the ceiling with his hands behind his head as if he hadn't heard her. He appeared to be deep in thought.

Katie was distracted from her irritation by the sight of his wide shoulders. Her mouth went dry as she ogled the stranger. Even through the linen shirt she could see he did more than computer programming or living a life of luxury. He had a rugged look to him that said he knew how to work with his hands and his body. Her eyes were drawn to the patch of bare skin exposed by the open V of his shirt then down to the waistband of his trousers. His tan pants looked as if they were part of a period costume but fit his long, muscular legs nicely.

The way he lounged on her bed with his legs spread across the coverlet made her think that he had no plans to leave anytime soon.

She mentally shook herself back to the situation. There was a man, although a very masculine and, well, let's face it, a downright yummy man, in her room. She didn't know him and she certainly hadn't invited him in.

"Uh, hello?" she said a little louder, trying to position herself behind the nearest chair, hoping to hide the fact that she wore very few clothes.

The man didn't even twitch.

"Hey! You there." Katie watched the man closely, looking for any kind of response but only saw a slight twitch in one foot. "Can you hear me?"

Either the man was deaf or he had earphones in. His reddish-blond hair had been tied back, giving her a clear view of one ear. There were no cords hanging down. *Perhaps he had a wireless device?* She hated to draw attention to herself given her lack of clothing but didn't believe she had another option since she had left her cell phone on the bedside table right next to the hotel phone.

She checked the area around her for something to toss onto the bed. If she could get the man's attention she'd simply point out he had entered the wrong room and he needed to leave. There were a few breakable trinkets on the bookshelf behind her along with, obviously, books. She spotted a small metal dish within reach. Since she wasn't sure how valuable any of the items were, she opted for the item least likely to break.

The bed was only fifteen or twenty feet away. *Surely she could Frisbee the dish onto the bed?* Maybe even make it land right next to the man. That should be enough to get his notice.

"Hey, Mr. Hunky Irishman! You need to get out of my room!" Katie said in a much louder voice. Still no response.

Okay. Katie stepped to the side of the tall-backed chair so she could leverage the dish properly. *Here goes nothing.*

The tarnished silver dish sailed across the span and landed on the foot of the bed as she planned. Thanks to the flat, smooth bottom, the dish skimmed across the bedspread and into the man lying on the bed.

Into the man. She blinked mutely.

Not up next to him.

Not bounced off.

Into the man.

Katie gaped at him, unsure of what she had seen. He looked real. He appeared to be corporeal. He didn't have the hazy, semi-transparent body that she associated with most spirits. But the dish had passed through him.

What the hell was he then?

As she stared, he turned his head and looked at her. Their eyes met. Katie's chest ached at the loneliness she saw in the depths of his gaze. Before she realized what she was doing she had stepped around the chair and moved toward him.

He sat up suddenly and asked, "You can see me, can't you?"

His native accent lent even more appeal to his deep, baritone voice. Even though she heard the faint echoey sound she associated with spirits, she had a very physical reaction. This was one of those rare men she would gladly listen to as he read stereo instructions.

Katie gave a slight, hesitant nod. She didn't like revealing her gift but figured her face and her reactions had already given her away.

The man jumped up and crossed the room quicker than she'd anticipated. With a squeak of alarm she darted behind the chair when he came to stand right in front of her.

"Who are you? And what are you doing in my room?" she demanded, pulling her courage around her like a cloak.

"Ah, lass, you have nothing to fear from me." He spread his hands out in front of him in a placating manner.

"I'll be the judge of that, thank you very much."

He tipped his head. "I apologize for startling you. It's been a good many years since someone other than the local specters could see or hear me. My excitement got the better of me."

"Yeah, well…" Katie stammered. "I can kinda understand that." She tucked a strand of hair behind her ear. "So, who are you?"

"Seamus MacDonhnaill." He made a short bow. "Formerly of the County Donegal MacDonhnaills."

"Formerly? Does that mean you got kicked out of that county or that family?"

He chuckled. The deep, rich sound sent ripples of warmth down to her core.

"Neither, actually." He cocked his head to one side and regarded her. "I have simply considered myself a resident of Tullamore Castle for some time now."

"Ah." The way he said resident make Katie think he did more than live here. She cleared her throat nervously. "I, uh… I don't want to be rude or anything, but I'm not comfortable standing here talking with someone I don't know when I'm only half- dressed."

Seamus' eyes quickly glanced down at the chair she had been using to keeping her modesty in place.

"Would you mind stepping out for a moment while I dig out a pair of jeans or something?" Katie asked. Seamus raised an eyebrow in question but Katie rushed on, "I know it's silly with you being…" Words failed her. Was Seamus a ghost? If so, he was unlike any she had come across before. "Uh, not quite solid, but I have a rule about being fully dressed when I meet new people."

Katie forced a smile on her face, even though she knew she had turned bright-pink from embarrassment.

To his credit, Seamus didn't laugh but he did a poor job of hiding his smirk. "Very well. When you're comfortable, simply open your door." Seamus moved to the door then paused and turned to look at her. With a mischievous grin he added, "I look forward to meeting you properly."

Katie frowned at Seamus' back as he passed through the closed door and disappeared from her sight.

She scampered to her suitcase and pulled out a clean pair of jeans. As she zipped them up it occurred to her that while she had demanded to know Seamus' name, she hadn't given him hers.

That had been very rude! Mom would have been appalled.

Shaking her head in disgust over her lack of manners, Katie dug in the pocket on the lid of her suitcase for a bra. She looked over her shoulder to where she's last seen Seamus, just to make sure he hadn't floated back in. Reassured that she still had the room to herself, Katie unwound the towel from around her hair and head then quickly pulled her shirt up and put her bra on.

Part of her wondered why she even bothered. After all, as a spirit, Seamus wouldn't be able to do anything other than look. A flash of warmth zipped down her spine at the thought that he would look.

Too bad he wasn't flesh and bone. She'd actually consider taking Jenny's advice if Seamus was the "hunky Irishman".

Now that she was fully dressed she felt less exposed. She went into the bathroom, grabbed her brush then she sat on the edge of the bed and debated the wisdom of inviting Seamus back in as she brushed the tangles from her hair. Yes, he knew she could see him but didn't know the extent of her gift. If he had an ounce of sense he'd ask, however. And right now, she didn't know what she'd tell him.

Why did Seamus appear different than other ghosts she had encountered? If that dish hadn't passed through him she wouldn't have realized he was a spirit. She needed to find out what he really was.

A picture of Seamus' face when he first looked at her popped into her mind's eye. In those brief seconds she had seen a loneliness so deep it created a knot in her chest when she recalled it. Had he really not talked with anyone other than a few ghosts in a long time?

She couldn't turn him away.

Besides, it wasn't as if he were pox-ridden with weeping sores or anything else disgusting. As a matter of fact, she found him a little too easy to look at.

Katie took a deep breath and released it. Her mind made up, she went to the door and swung it open. Disappointment rippled through her when she didn't find him waiting there.

She stepped out into the hallway and looked in both directions. The only thing she saw was a full set of armor standing guard a little ways down the hall, across from her room.

"Seamus?" Katie called quietly. She didn't hear a response or spot him anywhere. Where would he have gone? She shrugged and stepped back into her room, leaving the door ajar to let Seamus know he could come in if he returned.

With her head down, she didn't notice Seamus standing in the middle of the room until she practically ran into him.

"Jesus!" She jumped back in alarm. "Don't do that!"

"Do what?" Seamus asked even though a smiled played across his lips.

"Just… Just…" Katie shook her open hand in his direction to indicate she meant all of him. "Just show up like that. Can't you knock or something?"

"Actually—"

"Oh, never mind," she said, exasperated. Her heart raced from the startle and she struggled to get it under control. "I know you can't knock but you should announce yourself instead of just poofing in. Sheesh."

"Poofing? I don't think I have ever poofed in to anything." Seamus sounded somewhat insulted.

"Oh you know what I mean." Katie stomped over to the couch. "One minute you're not there and suddenly you are." She dropped onto her chosen seat then waved in Seamus' direction. "Poof."

"Ah. I see." He followed her to the sitting area and took a seat at the other end of the couch. "I'm guessing that I don't always manifest this state in a way that you can see me."

"This state?"

"Before I answer your obvious question, I believe that you owe me an introduction."

"Oh my God." Katie sat up straight on the couch. "I'm so sorry. I'm normally not that rude. My name is Katherine, well, Katie, to my friends, Ward. From America."

"Katherine Ward." Seamus smiled. "I had deduced by your accent that you are from the Americas. What brings you to Tullamore?"

Katie pulled her feet up under her. "I'm bringing my mother's ashes home."

Seamus dipped his head. "I'm sorry for your loss. Did she recently pass?"

"No. Actually she died about three years ago." At the questioning look in his eye she added, "I wasn't told of her request to be brought home to Ireland until a couple of weeks ago."

"Then I'm doubly sorry for your loss." He regarded her for a moment. "Your mother was Irish then." It was a statement more than a question.

"Yes."

"You do look like a daughter of Ireland." A frown creased his forehead as he continued to study her.

Katie squirmed nervously. "Did I suddenly sprout horns out of the top of my head?" she finally asked, uncomfortable with the way Seamus looked at her.

"You look like someone I've seen before." He absently rubbed his chin as he got lost in his thoughts once again. Then he shook his head as if to clear it and said, "I'll think of it later."

"If you say so," Katie mumbled. "So," she said brightly, changing the subject. "How did you come to be a spirit at Tullamore? Were you mortally wounded in battle on the castle grounds? Or did you fall off one of the castle walls during a siege? Or anything like that?"

Seamus' face darkened. Katie instinctively leaned back, away from the rage and disgust she saw in his eyes.

"I was cursed by a whore pretending to be a lady."

3

"CURSED?" Katie asked. Chills broke out across her skin. *Was he for real?*

Based on all her experiences with the odd and the unusual it she found it hard to dispute what he said, but the idea of someone being cursed horrified her.

Seamus nodded curtly. "Aye, cursed."

"So you were killed when the, er, when you were cursed?"

"I wasn't killed." At her wide-eyed stare he added, "I'm not dead."

"But..."

He shook his head, continuing to deny what she believed to be the truth.

"I can see you though," she insisted.

He crossed his arms over his chest. "You're one of the few who can."

"Yeah, but I see ghosts. You know, people who have died but their spirits haven't gone over to the other side? How is it that I can see you if you aren't dead?"

"You see people who are still alive too." He shrugged. "Maybe it's because I'm both. Or neither." He stood suddenly and raked his hand through his hair. "I'm not sure what I am. I haven't known for a great many years." His voice trailed off as he added, "Somewhere along the way I gave up trying to figure it out."

Katie's heart ached for him. It must be horrible living a half-life and not being able to interact with people the way he used to. She pulled her knees up to her chest and wrapped her arms around them. "What happened when you were... Well, when this curse went into effect?"

Her question jarred Seamus from his thoughts. He walked over to the window closest to the fireplace and looked out. "I was born in the year of our Lord, 1703."

Katie couldn't contain her gasp of surprise.

"When I was fourteen I apprenticed with a well-known woodcarver in a neighboring town. After I served out my apprenticeship I returned to Kilmorny to be near my family.

"My younger brother had died the previous year and my father was in poor health. Once I saw how much my mother needed me, I set out to find work. Lord Thomas Chichester held Tullamore back then and was working on one of the many expansions to the castle. I made an agreement with him for a few small carvings and once he saw my work, he decided to hire me exclusively for the work in the new section of the castle."

Katie shifted on the couch but Seamus didn't turn away from the window. She could only imagine how painful those memories were to dredge up.

"I spent a lot of time at Tullamore. Along with dozens of other local men who had been hired to work there. Unfortunately having that many able-bodied men behind the castle walls drew the attention of the Lord's much-younger and over-pampered wife Etain.

"Etain was a beautiful woman. She had very little trouble catching the eye of the men around her. And almost every man she lured to her bed went, whether they were married or not."

Seamus finally turned and looked at Katie. "Until me."

"You told her no?" she asked.

Seamus nodded.

"And she didn't like it," Katie guessed.

"No, she didn't." Seamus paced the width of the room. "At first she thought I was just trying to do right by his Lordship, but after repeatedly refusing her, she became angry.

"She tried telling me his Lordship would never know. Then she tried to make me feel sorry for her. More than once she hinted at how lonely it was living in the castle with nothing but servants because her husband was too busy doing things for the king or settling disputes between peasants."

At Katie's snort of disbelief, Seamus grinned. "She truly had a gift for weaving a sad story."

"I'm sure she did." Katie let her contempt show in each word.

"When she realized I wasn't falling for her story, she resorted to trickery. She followed me around, waiting for opportunities to corner me. She told me if I didn't do as she wanted, she would tell her husband I had attacked her."

"Damn. How desperate was she?" Katie exclaimed.

Seamus seemed surprised by Katie's outburst.

"Not that I'm surprised she'd want to sleep with you because, well, you..." Katie's face blushed scarlet. "I mean that you're so..."

She waved a hand in his direction but couldn't look him in the eye. "I'm just making a blunder of this," Katie muttered. She folded her arms across her chest and sank into the corner of the couch.

"How about if I just take that as a compliment and go on with my story, then?" Seamus asked with a quirk of his lips.

"Please do." Katie sulked.

"I found myself going to great lengths to make sure I was never alone with Etain. Any time she was around, if I couldn't leave immediately I had at least two other people nearby."

"That had to be annoying."

"To be sure," Seamus agreed. "But I needed the work and, in truth, I enjoyed putting my training to use." He raised his hand up in front of his face and curled his fingers into a fist then flexed them out again. "After all these years, I do miss working the wood," he said wistfully.

"I'm sure avoiding Etain drove her up the wall. What did she do?"

"It took a few decades to figure out, but I learned Etain went to the local wisewoman to purchase a love spell and ended up stealing her spell book."

"A wisewoman who sold love spells?" she asked with a lift of one eyebrow.

Shrugging one shoulder, Seamus said, "Wisewoman. Healer. Witch. They've been called many things. All I can tell you is that there have been generations of women who have lived in this area and have helped and even protected the people of Tullamore Castle with their extraordinary gifts."

"All women?"

"Yes. Apparently the abilities and the knowledge pass from mother to daughter. What few sons were born to these women had none of their gifts."

"What kind of gifts?" Katie's heartbeat sped up.

Seamus turned in her direction. "Stories have been told of the Mac au Bhaird for centuries. Most had a skill for growing herbs and for healing. Because of their close ties to Tullamore, they are able to sense when danger approaches. Some could even tell you what was going to happen. There were others that could supposedly control the weather."

Katie shivered as a chill passed through her. "Interesting," she mumbled. She didn't want to give anything away about her connection to the Mac au Bhaird family. She had only recently learned of it and still didn't know what to think. Perhaps once she'd met some of the family she'd feel better. If they had similar abilities to her and her mother, maybe she'd feel less like a freak. Katie shook free of her thoughts and asked, "So how did she put the spell on you? Say a few magic words and wave a wand? Or did she give you some kind of potion?"

"A potion, I'm afraid."

"How did she get you to drink it?"

"That was easy enough," he snorted. "She sent one of the kitchen maids with a tankard of drink to where I had been working. It was a warm summer day and I had gotten caught up in the carving I worked on. I thought it was full of spiced cider until after I had swallowed most of it."

Seamus began to pace again.

"You don't have to tell me the rest if you don't want to," Katie said quietly. "I can tell it bothers you."

"I don't mind the telling." He ran one hand through his hair and rubbed his forehead as if it ached right between his eyes. "It's difficult to sift through the gaps of what I remember about that day."

Once more Seamus returned to the window. "I remember thinking the drink tasted funny and that I'd been poisoned. My head swam and I tried to get help."

He stared out the window but Katie could tell he wasn't seeing anything outside. His focus remained on the scene playing out in his head.

"Everything got fuzzy and I collapsed before I could even get to the door. Next time I opened my eyes, Etain was kneeling next to me, telling me how she wished she didn't have to do it, but that I needed to say something. Something about her and me. Then I heard a woman screaming and a slap. When I opened my eyes again, Etain had the kitchen girl by the arm and was telling her to keep quiet or she'd be sorry. The girl was holding her cheek and crying. What was odd was she was looking at me and appeared to be more afraid of me than of Etain.

"When I reached for the girl, wanting to help her, she became even more frightened and backed away despite Etain's grip on her arm. That's when I noticed that I could see through most of my hand and arm."

"Oh God, Seamus," Katie whispered.

"I'm not sure what happened next. Etain said something but I didn't pay attention because I was trying to figure out what was happening to me. I remember thinking my body felt as if it were stuffed with wool and there was an odd tingling everywhere. I must have blacked out because the next thing I knew I was in a dark room with no candles or lamps.

"I stumbled around the room, trying to figure out where I was, but I was weak and my head felt as if I had been drinking the strongest ale made. It didn't take long to realize I couldn't feel things as I used to. As I lay on the floor, it no longer felt cold or hard. Just there, somehow. As I stumbled around the room I found no furniture in my path. When I tripped through the wall into the hallway with no impediment, I knew something was very, very wrong."

Seamus turned to look at Katie. She stared back, misty-eyed. She couldn't even imagine going through that without losing a little bit of sanity.

He walked to the couch and crouched down before her. "Why do you cry?"

"It's just not right that someone could do something like that to another person," Katie said emphatically. "To curse you to a pseudo-life for no reason. No reason other than her own greed."

Seamus reached up. Katie thought he would pass right through her in his attempt to try to wipe her tear away but something cool and tingly brushed her cheek instead. "What did you just do?"

"I..." Seamus looked at his hand. "I touched your tear." He rubbed his finger and thumb together. "And maybe your face." He sat back on his haunches.

"But I felt something. Something that felt cool and kind of buzzy." Katie absently patted the spot on her cheek where he had touched. "It was kind of like putting your tongue on the prongs of a nine-volt battery." When she got no response from Seamus she asked, "You've never done that, have you?"

He shook his head.

"Well, it's a weird feeling. Not painful. Just, well, weird. What did it feel like to you?"

"For the first time in hundreds of years, I felt warmth. It was, as you said, weird. And surprising."

"In all this time, you haven't felt warmth whenever you touched anyone else?"

"No. And believe me, I've tried a lot of different things, testing the limits of being a spirit. Some of those, quite frankly, were even done as a desperate attempt to end this existence."

He cocked his head to one side. "Would you mind if I tried it again, to see if it was just a chance occurrence?"

"You want to touch me again?" Katie sat up straight. "No. I mean, yes." A faint blush warmed her cheeks. "I mean I don't mind."

"Are you sure?" Seamus tried to hold back his grin but failed.

"Yes, I'm sure." She cleared her throat. "I'm, uh, curious. In the past, when I've come in contact with spirits, I have never felt anything other than chilled air."

Katie turned her face and leaned closer, basically presenting her cheek to him. "All right. Go ahead."

When he didn't move, Katie glanced at him from the corner of her eye. He seemed more interested in the freckles on her nose and cheeks than the tingles he'd felt.

"Did it work?" Katie prompted.

"I, uh, sorry. I got lost in a thought," he said, shaking off whatever he'd been thinking. He raised his hand to touch her and Katie saw it tremble just inches away from her face.

When they made contact, it surprised them both.

"Whoa." Katie's eyes widened but she didn't pull away. "There is definitely something there."

Seamus slid his hand up her cheek and into her hair.

"What does that feel like?" he asked Katie, his voice rough with emotion.

"It's... It's a cool, tingly feeling. Almost like the way peppermint feels."

"Peppermint." He ran his hand through her hair, following the strands down her shoulder and onto her arm. "So is that a good thing or a bad thing?"

"I, uh… It's definitely not a bad thing." Katie swallowed nervously. "What about you? You said you felt warmth?"

He looked up. "Not a great deal. But after hundreds of years of nothingness, even that bit of warmth is a blessing."

"How about if I try it?" "Try what?"

"Try touching you."

"Please do."

"Okay, sit back and close your eyes. I don't want you to anticipate feeling something. I'd rather know for sure you did."

"All right." He did as she asked.

Instead of his cheek, Katie tried to touch his chest where it had been exposed through his shirt. "Well?" she asked quietly.

"It's warm." Without opening his eyes he put his hand over the spot she touched. "Right here."

"So it's not just me."

He opened his eyes. "No."

For a moment their gazes locked and neither of them moved. Finally Katie said, "Okay then."

4

SO she had a spirit hanging out in her room. Never mind that he was as hunky as they came. He was not…well, solid. That was definitely important when deciding what she wanted in a boyfriend or a lover.

Not that she was looking for one.

On the positive side, since he was a spirit, there was very little he could do to harm her.

Then again, she already regretted that he couldn't lay those work-roughened hands on her. The frosty tingles were interesting but her girl parts were clamoring for more. And if Seamus kept looking at her the way he was right now—as if she were a well-stocked dessert buffet and he had been dieting for a decade—she was likely to make a complete fool of herself.

"Is there a way to break the curse?" Katie asked, hoping to change the direction of her thoughts.

"I think so. A few generations after the curse took hold I approached the local wisewoman and asked for help. Heloise was her name. She managed to locate Etain's diary and pieced together information from Etain's ramblings."

"What do you have to do to lift it?"

"I have to declare my love to the woman I am destined for."

Katie's heart skipped around in her chest. "That doesn't sound so bad."

Seamus' eyebrows lifted in question. "You think finding the one person that you were supposed to be with isn't hard?"

"Maybe. I mean, you have to believe in that sort of thing first."

"True," he agreed.

"Then you have to find that person."

"And how do you know that the person you found is really the person?"

"My mom used to tell me that the heart always knows."

Their eyes met. A warm sensation blossomed in Katie's belly and spread through her limbs.

"Perhaps your mom was right," he said quietly.

Katie blinked and tore her gaze away. She cleared her throat and asked, "So what ended up happening to Etain? I sincerely hope she didn't get away with cheating on her husband and putting curses on people."

"Nay." Seamus walked over to the window and looked out. "His lordship returned from his trip the morning after she burned my family's house and was given a full account of all that had transpired. Since no one could find me or my body, they assumed she had killed me and dumped my body somewhere it couldn't be found."

He took a deep breath. "She was hanged for murder not long after."

"Good."

Seamus' eyebrows shot up in surprise. "I didn't realize you were a bloodthirsty woman."

She crossed her arms over her chest. "Yeah, well, some people just need to be killed."

Her comment got a chuckle out of Seamus. "I suppose they do." Some of the tension left his face and shoulders.

"There's no other way to lift the curse?"

Seamus shook his head. "Heloise tried everything she could think of. She read journals, dug up old family stories and even offered to contact Etain on the other side."

"What about ghosts? Did you try talking with the local ghosts to see if they knew anything?"

"No. I don't have a lot of contact with the castle spirits. Most of them keep to themselves. The few I do talk to aren't easy to communicate with. It's like talking to them while being underwater." He froze with a strange look on his face. One that Katie was more than familiar with. It was the one that people wore when they thought she was either crazy or a freak of nature. "But you can, can't you?"

The way he drew out each word made her regret even bringing it up. "Maybe. I don't know for sure. Besides, there may not be any around."

She had to look away to tell that lie. There had been three spirits between the lobby and her suite and a dozen on the lawn when she first arrived. Given how big the Tullamore estate was, and with the amount of history connected to it, there were probably dozens more.

"Oh they're around all right," he confirmed. "Etain's spirit supposedly haunts one of the upper battlements overlooking the spot she died."

Chills ran down Katie's spine and across both of her arms. "Really?"

He nodded.

"Have you seen her?"

"No. And I don't want to either." He crossed himself. "I've heard the workers and guests both say she can be a bit moody. One day she's sad and complacent and the next downright hostile."

Oh good, crazy carries over into death. "Remind me to avoid that part of the castle," she mumbled. "This is going to be a total change of subject, but may I ask, out of all the rooms in the castle, what you were doing in this suite? You're not, like, some spirits that linger near where they died, are you?"

"I am not tied to this room. I can go wherever I want but I do feel a tie to Tullamore and haven't left the castle grounds for long periods of time." Seamus' gaze swept the room. "I don't know why I'm drawn to this room. Maybe because it is usually empty." He shrugged. "I am partial to the view of the gardens from here."

"Just wanted to make sure there isn't something weird about the room that I should know about. Like a dead body stuffed in the wall." She stood and walked to the window so she could take a look at the gardens outside. "After all, I'm going to be here for almost a month."

"Ah, well, you'll want to explore as much of the castle and the grounds as you can while you're here."

"Oh definitely. What I could see as we drove in was wonderful."

"If you'd like I could guide you around the castle and the grounds. I've been around long enough that I can offer a bit of insight into the castle's history."

"Do you think you could do it without making me look insane for talking to someone who isn't there?"

Seamus chuckled again. "I think we could manage that."

"The thing is..." Katie hesitated mentioning it, but it was important. "I don't want anyone to know I can see ghosts, much less communicate with them."

"Why not? There are lots of supernatural creatures around Tullamore. You don't have to worry about anyone here accusing you of being a witch or running you out of the village."

"Actually I'm more worried about people wanting me to try to contact their dead relatives. Or the ghosts wanting me to tell someone something or do something for them." She sighed. "I figured out a long time ago that I was better off pretending I didn't see things. People were less likely to treat me like a freak."

He nodded. "I can understand that. Heloise told me how people in the village treated her. Even though they came to her for help, there were some who wouldn't acknowledge her by the light of day."

"Exactly!"

"So why did you let me know you could see me?" Seamus asked with a tilt of his head.

"I, uh..." Katie stammered. She was not about to admit she had been stunned to find a gorgeous hunk lying in her bed after she had been fantasizing about something similar just moments before.

"Finding you here took me by surprise. I thought you were flesh and blood when I first saw you." She blurted out nervously, "You don't look like a ghost."

"I'm not a ghost."

"Well, no, you're not. But you're not quite, um, solid either."

"I am aware of that too," he mumbled.

"That must be rather difficult for you," Katie said. "To be trapped between worlds, so to speak."

"Some days more than others." He stood abruptly and walked to the suite door. "Then again, it does have its advantages," he said with a cocky grin.

Katie turned on the couch so she could watch where he went. "Like what?"

"I can peek at all the beautiful female hotel guests when they're in the bath and they don't even know it." Seamus winked at her then disappeared through the suite door.

"That's not ethical!" she shouted at the closed door.

Had he watched her while she took a bath? Or as she dressed or undressed?

A spiral of heat zipped through her body.

Another part of her became annoyed that he may have left in order to go watch some other unsuspecting guest.

Men!

No matter his reason, he'd be back. And when he did return, she would tell him exactly what she thought of his Peeping Tom activities.

5

AFTER tossing and turning for what felt like hours, Katie finally fell asleep. Strangely enough, once she did she slept deeply. Despite her vividly erotic dreams starring her and Seamus.

Her body still tingled from all the places she dreamed he had touched her. Too bad she left her vibrator at home. The horror of an airport security worker or a customs agent finding it lessened now that her hormones were on overload.

She rushed through her morning routine then dressed. Not just because of the likelihood of one spirit-like hunk popping in at any minute. The rumbling in her stomach and her anxiousness to see more of the castle spurred her.

Before heading out the door she grabbed her sweater and stuffed some money in her jeans pocket along with her door key. On her way to the lobby she took the opportunity to look at the paintings she'd passed the evening before.

One in particular caught her eye. It depicted a rocky coastline caught in a tempest. What made the portrait stand out was the lone figure standing atop a cliff looking out at the ocean. Even though it was small and barely noticeable, the long hair and billowing clothing hinted the shadowy figure belonged to a woman.

"I believe that is one of Brendan's works," Seamus said from behind her.

Katie had been so caught up in the painting, Seamus' sudden arrival didn't startle her. It didn't take long for the faint traces of ozone and wood to reach her. She now associated those two scents with Seamus.

"Brendan." Katie searched her memory banks, trying to place the name. "Is he the Irish artist who died mysteriously around here?"

"Something like that," he muttered.

Katie looked over at Seamus as he studied the painting. *What did he mean?* She returned her attention to the landscape. "His work is phenomenal. It evokes a great many emotions but I can't put my finger on why this one seems sad to me."

"Sad?" he asked incredulously.

"Yes. It looks to me as if the woman," Katie pointed at the shadowy figure on the right side of the painting, "is waiting for something. Or perhaps someone. And it feels as if she's been waiting for a long time." She turned to look at Seamus. "It makes me wonder if she ever found what she waited for?"

His arms were folded across his chest. "I'd like to think so."

Katie nodded then took one last look at the painting before continuing down the hall. None of the other paintings called to her enough to make her stop and study them but she did move slowly so she could look leisurely.

"Did you have a pleasant evening?" Katie asked.

"I did, thank you."

"I'm sure you did if you were off spying on unsuspecting guests." She didn't care if she sounded testy. Someone needed to show him how rude it was.

"Is that a hint of jealousy I hear in your voice, lass?"

Katie stumbled over her own feet. Jealousy? "What?"

Seamus chuckled. "That's what it sounds like."

"I am not jealous," she said vehemently. *Why would she be?* She'd only known him for a day.

The annoying man had the gall to shrug. "If you say so."

Katie opened her mouth to tell him exactly what she thought of his suggestion when a couple came into view, headed in their direction. Not only did she not want them to see her talking to thin air, she didn't want them to hear what she had to say to Seamus. Instead she kept walking and tried to ignore the ghostly figure floating beside her. His throaty chuckle made it hard to do.

"Good morning," the couple said as they passed.

"Good morning," Katie responded.

By the time the couple moved far enough away that Katie felt comfortable speaking again, she had decided she it would be better to not continue her previous line of thought. It would only encourage Seamus to pick on her further.

"So where can I find some breakfast around here?" she asked.

"Depends on what you're wanting. If you're a hearty eater, then you might want to try the main dining room. If you just want tea and toast then you might like the café near the lobby."

"How about something in between?"

"Marge's is just off the kitchens. What I've seen in there looks good."

"Oh I just realized. You don't eat, do you?"

"No, I don't."

"So how does that work, I wonder," Katie said aloud. "Every creature needs energy." She stopped in her tracks and looked at Seamus. "How do you sustain yours if you don't eat or drink?"

"Perhaps I should explain when we're not standing in a populated area. Unless you changed your mind about not letting people see you talk to yourself."

Katie looked around and saw they were standing in the main lobby. It was early enough that it wasn't busy but there were a few guests and hotel staff milling around.

"Oh." She felt her cheeks heat. "That would be better. Thanks."

She noticed several hallways leading from the lobby but nothing had been marked well enough for her to tell which direction she needed to go. Without looking at Seamus she asked quietly, "Which way?"

He pointed to a wide hallway on the other side of the room.

Katie tried not to watch as Seamus drifted through the furniture that she had walk around. It was a little weird to talk to him and see him act like a normal person then to see him do something ghostlike.

As she followed Seamus she wondered how long it took him to get used to his new physical form. Or lack thereof. It surprised her how many questions she had now that she had spent some time around someone who was basically a ghost. In the past she limited her contact with spirits and wouldn't let herself think about how they felt or what they experienced.

Odd how things change.

When they made it to the entrance of Marge's, Katie stopped and surveyed the area.

A waitress bustled by with a tray full of hot food. "You can sit wherever you'd like," she called out over her shoulder.

Seamus pointed to a table for two nestled off to one side, next to a window with a view of the gardens. "That should be out of the way enough so we can talk without drawing much attention."

Katie nodded once and headed in that direction.

A waitress came to the table just as she started to say something to Seamus. "Good morning. Do you need a menu?"

"Yes, please."

The waitress handed Katie a double-sided card. "Can I bring you tea or coffee while you decide what to order?"

Katie smiled up at the young lady. "Coffee, please. With cream and sugar."

"I'll be right back with that."

"Why did it sound as if you were asking for your favorite dessert?" Seamus asked as the waitress left.

Katie lowered her voice until the girl moved out of hearing range. "I have a deep appreciation for coffee. I have trouble getting my morning going without it."

Seamus leaned on the edge of the table and looked her directly in the eye. "I can think of other ways to get your morning started and none of them involve hot, bitter beverages."

Katie's jaw dropped and her mind was bombarded with a dozen pictures of the two of them lying naked in a bed. Sheets twisted. Limbs intertwined. Lips pressed against many different body parts.

She blinked to clear the images. "Stop that!" she whispered harshly.

The man had the audacity to grin. "Stop what?"

"You know exactly what—"

"Ma'am, did you need something?" one of the other waitresses asked as she stopped at their table. "I can call your waitress for you."

"Oh... I, uh... No. I'm fine, thank you." Katie's cheeks grew hot and were most likely bright-red.

At least the waitress didn't look at her as if she had grown a second head before she walked away.

"You're doing that on purpose, aren't you?" Katie growled.

"Doing what?" Seamus chuckled.

"First you distract me with suggestive images. Then you make me forget where I'm at and embarrass me in front of the waitress." Even to Katie's own ears she sounded whiny.

His voice dropped. "What sort of suggestive images did you

see, lass?"

"I—" Katie stopped herself. "That's none of your business."

"Here's your coffee, ma'am," the waitress said as she set the pot near the center of the table.

Thank God. Coffee. And an interruption before she said something really embarrassing.

Katie smiled gratefully at the waitress. "Thank you very much."

"You're welcome." The waitress set a coffee cup and saucer on the table in front of Katie. "Are you ready to order?"

"Oh, no. I'm sorry, not yet."

"Take your time. I'll return in a wee bit." The waitress went to check on the other guests a few tables away.

Without even glancing at the menu Katie reached for the coffee. "It's weird to sit here and make myself a cup of coffee knowing it's pointless to offer you any."

"Thank you for the thought anyway." Seamus cocked his head to one side. "It's been so long since I've eaten anything I don't remember what most things taste like so I don't really miss it anymore."

Katie's heart lurched in her chest.

"I remember enjoying certain foods. But I don't remember exactly why I did."

"That's just so unfair, Seamus. You shouldn't have to live like that."

He shrugged. "But I am. And there's nothing I can do about it."

"Well," Katie's voice trailed off. There was nothing to be done about it. At least not right that minute.

After breakfast they headed to the front lobby. Katie wanted to grab a few brochures and see what kinds of tours were offered. She was a little tired but had no intention of sitting in her room. There was too much she wanted to see in Ireland.

"You know, lass, I can show you around the castle and the grounds."

"Yes, I'm sure you can. And you probably have an interesting perspective on the history of both. But, no offense, I'd like to be able to interact with more people than just you."

"Ah. So it's a man you're wanting to meet, then?"

"What?" Katie stumbled then recovered her feet. "No! I mean, why would you think that?" She felt her cheeks get warm.

"You're an attractive, unmarried woman. I haven't heard you

talk to, or talk about, a man back home. Why would you not want to, how do they say it these days? Hook up with a man?"

Forgetting about her promise not to acknowledge Seamus' presence whenever they were in public, Katie stopped and put her fists on her hips. "Now you listen here. Just because I don't have a boyfriend right now doesn't mean that I am on the hunt for one. I have been managing just fine without one for well over a year now."

"Well, dearie, if you haven't had a man in over a year and now you're standing in the middle of the hallway talking to yourself, you might want to rethink your plan to find one." The unsteady voice of an elderly woman floated over Katie's shoulder.

With her cheeks flaming-hot, Katie turned to find a little, white-headed woman with twinkling eyes standing behind her.

"I, uh—"Mortification settled in Katie's gut making her unable to form a reply.

"I'm sure one of the braw Irish lads wandering about these parts," the woman waved her cane in the direction of the lobby, "would be just the thing for you." She winked and added, "Might even get your lady parts in working order again too."

Katie's jaw hinged open.

"If you can't run one to ground by week's end, give me call and I'll find you one." The old woman continued to the restaurant but called over her shoulder, "Have the front desk ring Ms. Peggy."

As soon as Katie's brain began functioning again she whirled around to confront the source of her irritation. "You! You…"

"What did I do?" Seamus asked, pretending innocence as he tried, and failed, to smother his laughter.

"I… You… She…" Katie sputtered. "Oooh, I knew it was a bad idea to talk to you." She stomped into the lobby mumbling unpleasant things about men in general.

Without looking, she knew Seamus had followed her.

Just because she hadn't had sex in over a year didn't mean that her lady parts weren't working. She wasn't above using her vibrator when she needed to. Or her hands. She didn't need a man.

Yes, they were nice to have around sometimes. They were usually warm. And she was quite fond of being snuggled up against a broad, masculine chest. She didn't even mind feeling the weight of a lover sprawled upon her.

She stopped when she reached one of the seating areas in the lobby and sighed.

If she was completely honest with herself, she did miss having a man in her life. But that didn't mean she needed to rush right out and grab the first one she stumbled across.

Seamus slipped past Katie and slumped into the nearby chair. He must have sensed her mood and wisely kept his comments to himself.

Really, it was too bad that Seamus was a spirit. She enjoyed his company. When he wasn't embarrassing her, that is. And he was certainly easy to look at. Her supposedly unused lady parts took notice anytime he came around.

If only...

Looking across the lobby, Katie spotted a couple locked in a sensual embrace. While the man was handsome, his rugged good looks and bare chest were not what caught her attention. It was the fact that he was semi-transparent, a telltale sign that he was a ghost, but the woman wasn't.

It took a moment for it to register with Katie that the man was kissing and fondling the woman and, based on the woman's reaction, she could feel more than tingles where they touched. As a matter of fact, it looked as if the woman was enjoying what he was doing very much.

Katie tore her gaze away. The first thing she saw was Seamus. He was watching her closely.

Remembering the embarrassing scene with the woman in the hallway, Katie moved closer to the chair Seamus occupied and lowered her voice. "Can you see the couple directly across from us?"

"I only see a dark-haired woman in a purple dress with something shimmering around her. I'm guessing that watery figure is a ghost?"

"Yes, I believe so."

"Is he doing something to her right breast?"

Katie took another quick glance. "Yes, he is."

"She seems to like whatever he's doing," Seamus observed.

"Um, yeah, I think so," Katie said as her cheeks turned warm. "My question is, how is he able to do that where she can feel it?"

Seamus took more interest. "I'm not sure," he said slowly. "Describe him to me."

"Well... He has brown hair. It's kind of long and wavy. No

shirt, just black pants. Based on how much he's bent over and how large his hand looks on her, I'd guess he's quite tall."

"Thin or fat?"

"Definitely not fat. Just a lot of muscle."

Something about her answer made Seamus grumble. He got up, walked over to the couple and looked closer at what the man was doing. He did stay far enough away to not interrupt. Thankfully Seamus' presence didn't disturb either the man or the woman.

"Interesting," Seamus said when he returned to where Katie stood.

"What is?"

"He is definitely touching her and she definitely feels him."

"But how is that possible?" She glanced back at the couple. "I've run into hundreds of ghosts and I don't feel much more than cold air. My contact with you is the exception," she amended. "Most people don't even know ghosts are there."

"I don't know," Seamus said with a thoughtful look on his face. "But I will be finding out."

When their eyes met a flare of heat erupted low in her belly. She swallowed hard and tried to ignore the images that popped into her head of the two of them together.

"So!" she said a little brighter and louder than intended. "What say we find those brochures?"

6

THE tour of the castle had been enlightening. Seamus made even the mundane details interesting. And, in truth, Katie enjoyed his company. Before even getting on the airplane she had worried how she'd spend three weeks in a foreign country all alone.

At least she wasn't completely alone.

Seamus seemed to enjoy having someone to talk with also. Katie couldn't imagine spending hundreds of years with nothing to do and few people to interact with.

Now that she'd had a nap she was anxious to see the gardens that lay outside her suite windows. She pulled a sweater from the armoire and headed to the lobby. Katie was sure she had passed some French doors in one of the hallways off the lobby that looked as if they led to the gardens.

On the stone patio just outside the French doors, Katie took in how extensive the gardens were. As she passed through the archway marking the entrance to the gardens, Seamus materialized next to her. Thankfully his sudden appearance no longer startled her.

"Good evening. Were you able to rest?" Seamus asked.

"Indeed. What about you?"

"In my own way, yes."

Katie stopped walking and looked at Seamus. "I wondered about that. Do you sleep?"

He frowned. "I don't sleep the way I did before the curse. But I do rest, if you will. A couple hundred years ago I learned how to conserve my energy so I wouldn't just fade out without warning."

"What do you mean without warning?"

"When the curse first took hold of me, I would black out for

39

periods of time." He shrugged. "Sort of like falling asleep suddenly."

"Seriously?" Katie became angry again for what Etain did to Seamus.

"After a while I realized it was similar to falling asleep after working in the fields or over an intricate carving for too long. Your body just stops when it's had enough."

Katie resumed her stroll in the direction of the gardens. "I suppose it takes energy to exist no matter what form the body is in. If you can't eat to create energy, then I suppose you'd have to recharge your batteries somehow."

"That's the conclusion I came to as well." They shared a smile. "I also noticed," Seamus continued, "that whenever I made myself visible to someone, I required more, what did you call it? Recharging?"

"So you can choose to make yourself visible to people?"

"Somewhat. I've been told it's not a solid form. I'm guessing it's the kind of thing that creates many of the current ghost stories."

"Interesting."

They came to a wall of shrubbery.

Katie looked to her left and then to her right but didn't see an opening through the thick hedges. She tilted her head in Seamus' direction. "So how do I get in?"

"To the maze?"

"They have a garden maze? I didn't notice that from my window. I just thought the wall hid a well-manicured garden."

"There are a lot of things at Tullamore that are not as they appear."

Katie studied Seamus' expression but couldn't detect anything out of the ordinary. But she felt certain he was hiding something from her. "Like what?"

"If we come across it I'll tell you. How about that?"

"Harrumph." She waved to the shrubbery wall. "So tell me about these gardens."

"They are the finest example of Irish horticulture you'll find in this county."

"Really? So how do I get in?" Katie tried to keep the exasperation out of her voice.

Seamus looked up at the sky, specifically in the direction the sun was setting. "Are you sure you wish to see this so late this evening?

The sun will be set in less than an hour."

"That's okay. I didn't plan to stay long. Just wanted to stretch my legs a bit."

"If I show you the way to the entrance, will you promise to stay close to the front entrance and leave if I tell you to?"

"What? Why?"

"Because it's going to be dark very soon."

"So?"

"I would feel better if you were not out here after the sun sets."

"Is there something out there I should worry about?"

"Let's just say there will probably be some things in the garden you won't want to see."

"Like what? Pagan rituals? Werewolves hunting prey?"

"The weres tend to stick to the woods at night, so no."

"Okaaaaay," she said hesitantly. "Unless there's something out here that is an immediate threat to my life, how about if you let me be the judge of whether or not I want to see it? And if I do see something I don't want to see, I'll chalk it up to, 'you were right', and I'll turn around and leave."

"As you say."

"Now. Which way should I go to get into the garden?"

"There is an entrance about fifty meters that way."

Katie walked in the direction Seamus indicated. "Well, what do you know?" she mumbled when she found the gate.

If someone were standing directly across from the entrance they would see it. But because the wood gate had been set into the middle of the shrubbery thickness, it was not noticeable.

Inside the garden there were pathways made with rock stepping-stones. Patches of grass grew between the blocks, making it appear as a level walkway. Shrubbery lined the outside perimeter and was also scattered around the extensive gardens.

Nothing was blooming but even without a multitude of spring colors the gardens were beautiful. Whoever designed the area had been quite imaginative. They created cozy nooks where visitors could relax in the sun, nap in the shade or simply escape from the world.

Sculptures were scattered throughout in various shapes and sizes. The tiny ones added a touch of whimsy. The life-sized reminded Katie of the ancient Greek statues she'd seen in museums.

One statue brought Katie to a halt. She speculated how any man with that size of, um… equipment would either make some woman extremely happy or rather uncomfortable.

After wandering through the garden with Seamus, Katie found a secluded spot that appealed to her. She curled up on one of the cushioned lounge chairs she found tucked into a corner. As she settled herself she noticed the chair had been made unusually large. Two people could fit side by side on the lounge but without much elbow room.

Seamus perched at the end and watched the last few rays of the sun dip below the horizon.

"Do you watch many sunsets, Seamus?"

"No." He hesitated then added, "There was a time when I did."

"What changed?"

The look he shot her said she was being a simpleton.

"Your curse?" She frowned. "Why would being cursed take away your enjoyment of something like the beauty of nature?"

He looked in the direction of the setting sun but Katie could still see the expression on his face. The pain there made her heart ache. "I've seen hundreds—probably thousands—of sunsets. Somewhere along the way I realized I'd probably see a thousand more. None of them bringing any peace or relief from this dreary existence. None of them any different than the last. Finally I quit watching them."

She ached to comfort him but didn't know how. There were no words she could say to make it right so she sat with him and let the quiet of the garden envelop them.

As Katie and Seamus sat in silence, enjoying the peace of the evening, Katie noticed noises coming from the other side of the surrounding trellis. She thought she heard two voices, male and female. What caught her attention was the male voice ordering the person with him to strip.

Startled and unsure she had heard correctly, she looked at Seamus. Instead of being shocked or embarrassed, Seamus watched her, as if waiting to see what she would do.

Katie pointed in the direction of the voice and mouthed, "Did he really say that?"

Seamus stood and glided to the part of the trellis that separated them from the voice on the other side. "Come and see for yourself."

Katie's jaw hinged open. *She wasn't going to peek through the shrubbery!* Especially if the couple on the other side had taken their clothes off. She shook her head.

"Lovely," the unknown male voice said. "I love looking at your breasts. If I had my way, you would never cover them."

Seamus shamelessly peered through the greenery.

"Yes, my Lord," the female said demurely.

"Do you know what I love better than looking at your breasts?" the male voice asked.

"No, my Lord."

"I love looking at your pussy." Seamus looked at Katie.

She was thankful for the shadows so Seamus couldn't see how red she had probably turned. Katie gestured for Seamus to come closer, away from the trellis, then pointed in the direction of the alcove exit. There were private things happening on the other side of the trellis that shouldn't be disturbed.

Seamus held out his hand. "You asked what I did to amuse myself over the years."

Katie looked at the trellis then at Seamus, then back at the trellis.

"You amused yourself by watching people have sex?" she whispered.

"Sometimes."

"Seriously?" Her question came out as a quiet squeak.

Seamus lifted one shoulder in a half-shrug then turned back to the couple on the other side.

Why were people fascinated by watching other people? She'd read dozens of magazine articles that said guys were easy to stimulate visually. Watching another couple during an intimate encounter seemed like an invasion of privacy.

At the same time, the idea intrigued her.

Seamus looked at her once again. Katie wondered if he had read her mind when he held out his hand and beckoned her to his side.

She took a deep breath then crossed the short distance to where Seamus stood. Her body tingled where it brushed against his energy. Seamus must have felt it too because he backed up to give her room.

"All right. What's the big deal?" she asked softly.

"Take a quick look." He pointed at a spot in the trellis where the leaves were thin. "Just a brief look, then tell me what you saw."

After a fortifying breath, Katie centered her eye over the opening. Most of the seating area on the other side could be seen through the small space.

"Okay, look at me."

Katie turned her gaze away from the couple on the other side and focused on Seamus.

"What did you see?"

"I, uh…" Keeping her voice low, she said, "I saw a man, sitting on the stone bench, and a woman kneeling on the ground in front of him."

"How were they dressed?"

Katie's cheeks grew warm. "She didn't look dressed at all. At least not that I could see." She frowned as she tried to remember. "I think the man still had all of his clothes on, but I couldn't tell you what he wore. He sat too far into the shadows."

"What were they doing?" Seamus asked.

"I'm not sure. It kind of looked like he was petting her," she answered quietly.

"And how did you feel as you watched them?"

Katie shifted her stance. "Uncomfortable."

"Is that all?"

"What do you mean?" she asked, keeping her voice low.

"Were you repulsed by what you saw?"

"No."

"Did it excite you?"

Katie had to stop and think about it.

"Be honest, Little Katie. There is no reason you shouldn't tell me."

She ducked her head. "Maybe a little bit," she reluctantly admitted. When she looked up at Seamus she added quietly, "I wouldn't say I was turned on in the same way a passionate kiss can do. Intrigued would be a better word for it."

Seamus nodded. "Are you intrigued enough to see more?"

Katie looked at the trellis, imagining what might be happening on the other side. She shrugged. "Maybe." She turned back to Seamus. "I guess you don't see this as an invasion of privacy, huh?"

"Not when the couple has chosen a public place for their tryst. Couples who engage in these kinds of displays are often excited by the possibility of being caught or of someone seeing them."

"So you're just obliging them then?" she asked, wishing she

didn't have to remember to keep her voice down while Seamus didn't.

"Perhaps."

"I suppose that's one way to look at it," she mumbled as she turned to look through the vines again.

Seamus chuckled.

The couple on the other side must not have noticed Katie's whispered conversation. Either that or they didn't care that someone might be watching. They continued their interlude with no interruption.

The man had bound the woman's hands behind her back. She stood before him with her legs spread wide enough for him to have complete access to all of her. He said something and the girl nodded in response. The man slowly circled the woman. His hands skimmed across her naked body in various places, evoking a quiver or a gasp in response.

When he pinched the woman's nipples Katie's own breasts perked up and tingled. She wondered what it would be like to be in the woman's place. To desire someone enough that she would be willing to stand in a garden, completely naked, and allow him to do these things to her. To let herself be bound, making touch almost one-sided.

A shiver of awareness ran through Katie's entire body.

"I think she likes it," Seamus said softly.

"Wha—" Katie pulled her eyes away from the couple. "What makes you think that?"

"The way her breath catches. The somewhat dazed expression on her face. The movement in her pelvis whenever he touches a sensitive spot."

Seamus' gaze danced over Katie's face, making her hyperaware of his notice.

"If it were lighter out, we would be able to see how flushed she is," he added. "And if we were closer we would probably even be able to smell her arousal."

Katie's heartbeat stepped up its tempo.

"Do you really think so?" she asked, barely remembering to keep her voice down.

"I can float over there and find out for sure," he offered.

"No, don't go," she answered quickly then dropped her voice to a whisper once again. "I mean, there's no need to risk disturbing them."

He held her gaze for the longest time, or at least it felt long to Katie. Finally he returned his attention to the couple on the other side.

Katie peeked through the space in the trellis.

The man had moved in close to the woman. His chest probably brushed the back of her shoulder when he asked, "Do you know why I brought you here?"

"No, my Lord."

"Oh I think you do."

"To fuck me, my Lord?"

"That's right."

A shiver ran through the woman.

Katie felt a similar one run through her body.

The man untied the woman's hands. "But not just yet." He walked around the woman and sat on the bench in front of her. "You're going to have to prove to me that you're ready to be fucked."

"May I touch you, my Lord?"

The man leaned against the wall behind the bench and let his knees fall open. "Proceed."

Katie turned to Seamus and whispered, "Why is she asking for permission to touch him? If they're a couple wouldn't she normally do that?"

One side of Seamus' lips curved upward. "They aren't what you would think of as a traditional couple." He paused. "At least, not here, in this moment."

Katie waited for him to continue.

"You have heard of Doms and subs, haven't you?"

"You mean like a dominatrix?" she asked a little louder than intended.

"The dominant personality in a Dom-sub or Master-slave relationship."

"Is that what's going on over there?" Even with her voice low, it squeaked in surprise.

"It's just a wee bit of play, that's all." He shrugged. "Tomorrow you may see them at breakfast or strolling the grounds like any other couple."

"Hmmm." Katie fell mute. She'd heard of couples who did that sort of thing but had never thought about whether or not the idea might interest her. The idea of witnessing it in action was almost too much.

As she turned back to the couple she said a prayer of thanks that Seamus didn't question her about her lack of experience or judge her for it.

The woman on the other side knelt at the man's feet, between his knees. It looked as if she had unfastened the man's belt and now worked on his zipper. The man leaned further back against the wall, putting his face in the shadows, which made it hard to see his reaction.

At least she could see one part of him. And that part seemed to enjoy everything the woman did including being freed from the confines of the man's pants.

And what an impressive part it was.

Katie didn't have a lot of experience with men but none of them had the girth this man had.

"Wow," she blurted, not meaning to say it out loud.

"No man wants his sword compared to others but even I have to say that is unusually large."

Katie's cheeks heated. She couldn't look in Seamus' direction. Instead she focused on what the woman was doing to the man.

The woman took the man's oversized cock in hand and stroked it in a slow, rhythmic motion. Then she leaned in and licked it from the bottom to the top. As she did, her free hand roamed across the man's chest and over his abs.

When the woman began licking in earnest and finally took it all into her mouth, Katie became hyperaware of Seamus' presence beside her.

While she became a bit of a turn-on watching the other couple, she felt somewhat smutty for eavesdropping.

"I, uh—" Katie stuttered. "Perhaps I should get back to the hotel."

Seamus looked at her. For some reason, she wondered if he were peering into her soul.

"You don't want to see how this ends?" he asked.

"I would hope it ends with the expected outcome." She smiled, hoping to ease some of the tension sparking between them.

"Most likely," he said with a nod. "But it's the journey there that makes the trip worthwhile."

Katie tilted her head to the side. "That's true."

"So why are you running away, Little Katie?" Seamus' voice dropped to a husky tone that made Katie's insides quivery.

"I'm not running away. I'm just trying to give these guys some privacy."

"Hmmm," Seamus said noncommittally as he searched her face and eyes. "Did it make you uncomfortable to watch them?"

"A little."

"I would have been surprised if it hadn't."

"Then why did you suggest that I do?"

"Because you need to find out for yourself whether or not you can and if it's something that you'd like to try." He paused. "One of the reasons I began watching couples around Tullamore was so I could pretend, for a little while, I was the one doing those things. To remember what it was like to touch a woman's skin."

Seamus lifted his hand to Katie's face. She felt the electric tingles across her cheek where his fingertips brushed her skin. When she met his gaze, the pain and longing she saw renewed the ache in her chest. The need to comfort him and chase away the cold and loneliness overwhelming her.

"It helps me remember the pleasure that can be found in the arms of a woman."

"Do you remember? After all this time?" she asked.

"Yes." His fingers drifted down the side of her face and neck then across the curve of one breast. "Yes, I do."

The tingles she felt where he touched her sent a wave of heat and desire through her body. Her lips fell open on a gasp. "You know I can feel that, don't you?"

Even in the darkened alcove, she could see desire burning in his eyes. "What do you feel, Little Katie?" His finger returned to her breast and hovered over the area where her nipple remained tucked inside her bra and shirt.

The husky sound of his voice sent another wave of heat through her body.

Maybe it was because they had just watched something very intimate together, or she needed to ease some of Seamus' pain, or perhaps she was surprisingly comfortable with Seamus. Whatever the reason, she found the courage to answer him.

"When you touch me, I feel tingles, like an electric current." She closed her eyes to focus on the feeling of his hand on her skin. "But there is also coolness."

Dena Garson

"It is not unpleasant?"

"No." She shook her head then opened her eyes. "As a matter of fact, it is a little stimulating."

"I see." He skimmed his other hand across her other breast. Familiar tingles then another flash of heat raced through her belly.

"Shall we try something else, then?"

"Like what?" she asked, drawing each word out.

"You watch." He pointed to the trellis. "I'll stand behind you and you tell me what you feel."

She didn't know what he planned but the possibilities excited her. "Okay," she said softly then positioned herself so she could see through the trellis.

The air moved around Katie as Seamus shifted to stand behind her. The expected coolness and tingling zipped up and down her body where he brushed against her. She wrapped her fingers through the slats of the trellis to steady her wobbly knees but couldn't help looking over her shoulder to where he stood. The smell of wood and ozone permeated her senses. She breathed deeper, taking as much of it in as she could.

Her fingers twitched from the need to caress his bristly cheek.

"Look," he said gently with a lift of his chin, directing her to the couple on the other side.

It was an effort to drag her eyes away from his face.

When she did she saw the woman standing in front of the man with her legs straddling his knees. Since he was reclined, it put her crotch just below his eye level.

One of his hands held her by the hip. The other worked her clit in slow, easy strokes. He spoke to her but based on how the woman's head rolled back, she probably couldn't pay attention to anything except his fingers on her pussy.

As Katie watched she became aware of a tingling sensation on and around her own pussy. She swallowed hard and tried to focus on what she could see through the trellis.

The tension building in the woman became more obvious. Her muscles were rigid, her lips were parted and Katie could hear her panting.

"What do you think she's thinking right now?" Seamus whispered near Katie's ear.

"Probably, 'Dear God don't stop'," Katie whispered back.

49

Seamus' chuckle made her smile but her gaze didn't waver. "What about you? What are you thinking right now?"

Katie's cheeks warmed. "That I am getting more turned-on than I expected."

"How do you know? What are you feeling?"

Katie turned her head to look at Seamus but he stopped her. "No. Don't stop watching. Stay focused on them."

She did as he asked.

"Tell me what you feel," he urged.

"I, uh… I'm warm."

"Why?"

"Probably because I'm both embarrassed and turned-on," she admitted.

"What else?"

"My breasts feel heavy. It's kind of like the fabric of my bra is irritating them."

"Do you want to take it off?"

"What, my bra?" she asked, a little shocked by the idea.

"That and maybe even your blouse too."

Katie's mouth hung open. She had to make herself sort through the conflicting feelings and thoughts being scrambled around inside her.

"I… No." Katie paused. "Sort of. But mostly no." She found herself needing to explain. "It would definitely be more comfortable without the bra or shirt," she whispered, "but I wouldn't be comfortable being out here without clothes."

"I understand." Seamus took a small step back. "I find myself uncomfortable with the idea of another man seeing you even partially undressed." He ran his finger down her spine, making Katie stand up tall. She sucked in a breath through her now-clenched teeth.

"What are our friends on the other side doing now?" Seamus asked, even though he could look for himself.

"He's licking her down there," she whispered.

"Down where?" Seamus pushed.

She hesitated before she answered. "Between her legs."

"Does it look as if she likes it?"

"I would say so."

"What about you, Little Katie? Do you like it when your lover does that to you?"

She swallowed hard. "Yes."

"Did he make you come when he did it?"

Her voice deserted her. She nodded reluctantly. Why did she feel compelled to answer his very personal questions?

Her world stilled when she realized the answer.

Because she trusted him.

They hadn't known each other long but she did.

"Would you like to come now?" he asked.

"I…" She squirmed and transferred her weight to her other foot but it still didn't alleviate the throbbing in her pussy. Her now-damp panties certainly didn't help her situation.

"No," she told him. "Not yet."

"If I could, I would slip my hands into your pants so I could see how ready you really are."

Seamus' silky-smooth voice ran through her like a caress. The images he created in her mind pushed her closer to passion's edge. If he were able to touch her, it probably wouldn't take him long to help her get to that much-needed orgasm.

"You are wet, aren't you, Little Katie?"

She shuddered when she felt tingles on her ear as well as her butt cheek and hip. "Yes."

Finally the woman on the other side of the trellis threw her head back and yelled out her release. Her body shivered and convulsed as the man held her by the hips and drank in her nectar.

Katie's breath caught. She remained transfixed by what she had seen.

Suddenly the man stood, grabbed the woman by the waist and switched places with her. He flipped the woman around and bent her over, forcing her to grab on to the seat of the bench. Holding her by the hip with one hand, he guided his cock into her pussy.

He pushed in as far as he could go and held that position for a moment. Both of them looked as if they were savoring the feeling.

When the man eased back then quickly rocked forward, Katie's own pussy clenched in response. The man's rhythm picked up and soon he was pounding into the woman, their bodies making slapping noises when they came in contact.

"Touch yourself," the man told the woman. "I want to feel you come on my dick."

Katie couldn't tell from where she stood but the woman must have complied because her moans became louder. Finally the woman let out a hoarse cry. The man answered by thrusting into her a couple more times before stiffening and grunting with his own release.

Katie groaned. The visual stimulation had become too much.

"Seamus," she pleaded, even though she wasn't sure what she was asking for.

"I'm here, Little Katie," he reassured her. "What would you ask of me?"

"I don't know," she whispered as she turned away from the trellis. "I need…"

"What do you need?" he pressed.

Her body trembled. "I need you to touch me." She tried to keep her voice low. "I need to come, Seamus."

He stepped closer. "If I could, I would lay you on that lounge, spread your legs and make you come as I buried myself in you."

Katie shivered in response.

"But since I can't, you're going to have to do most of the work. Go sit on the lounge."

She did what he told her.

"Lie back and slip your pants off."

"Um. I don't think that is a good idea," she whispered and pointed to the trellis that shielded them from the other couple.

He shrugged. "Then just loosen the fastenings."

Katie looked around to see if anyone could see her. There were enough shadows to make it unlikely. Then again, she just spent the last half hour watching the couple on the other side of the trellis. With as little traffic as she saw in the gardens when they walked in and the fact that the sun had almost completely set, Katie felt it was reasonably private.

She unbuttoned her jeans and pushed the zipper down.

"Now, slip your hand in and tell me how wet you are."

Once again she did as Seamus bade. Her fingers skimmed through the narrow patch of hair until she reached her clit. She pushed past the swollen nub until she reached what her fleshy folds were trying to hide.

"Very."

She drew the silky dampness up to her clit then slid her finger back and forth across the sensitive peak. Katie bit her lip as she absorbed the sensation. Knowing Seamus watched heightened the feeling.

Their gazes locked as she rubbed her clit with slow, steady strokes.

In her mind's eye she saw Seamus leaning over her. It was his hips that pushed her legs open. It was his hand that touched her pussy. It was his finger that stroked her clit.

The sound of crunching gravel startled Katie out of her fantasy.

Seamus put one finger to his lips, telling her to remain silent, then floated through the trellis wall. Katie zipped and buttoned her jeans and straightened her top.

When Seamus returned he said, "It's just a couple out for a stroll."

Katie nodded. "Perhaps we should get back to the room."

"If you'd like."

"You're coming too, right?" she asked as she stood.

"Is that a trick question?" He smirked.

Katie snorted in response. "Oh whatever." She brushed past Seamus so he wouldn't see her cheeks turn even more pink.

As they walked back to the garden entrance, they passed a couple walking arm in arm. A pang of jealousy struck Katie. If things were different, she would be strolling in the garden with Seamus' arms around her. Then again, if things had been different, she would have never met him.

7

"ARE you all right?" Seamus asked.

"I'm fine. Why?"

"You have an odd look on your face."

"I do?" Katie pretended innocence.

He nodded. "Either you had an unpleasant thought or you need to go to the bathroom. Care to tell me which it is?"

Katie laughed. "Well, I don't need to go to the bathroom."

"Then what thought made you frown?"

She smiled, amazed by his perception. "It occurred to me that if things had been different, I would have never met you."

It was his turn to look pensive. "I suppose that's true."

"Not that I'm glad you had a curse placed on you or anything," she reassured him. "I wouldn't wish that on anyone."

"I wouldn't think so."

The walk back to the garden entrance didn't take as much time since they didn't weave in and out of the many pathways. As they climbed the steps to the terrace, they fell silent. Several couples were milling about. Katie guessed they were either having drinks before dinner or relaxing after.

"Are you hungry?" Seamus asked. He must have noticed all the people in the hall outside the restaurant as well.

She shook her head without saying anything. She ate lunch late and wasn't ready for dinner just yet so they kept moving to Katie's room.

After unlocking the door, she held it open for Seamus. As he floated by she realized how pointless the gesture had been but ingrained habits were hard to break. Not that she frequently let men into her hotel room.

"So…" she said as they reached the sitting area.

"The night air was a bit cool. Did you get chilled?" Seamus asked.

"A little."

"How about a bath to warm you up again?" he suggested.

Katie smiled. "That's not a bad idea."

The bathroom was probably the best thing about the suite. The blend of modern conveniences and antique designs created a relaxing atmosphere.

She went immediately to the tub, pulled the stopper and turned on the hot water. When she turned around she found Seamus leaning against the counter with his arms folded over his chest, watching her.

A thrill shot through her as she thought about stripping in front of him. Could she really do it?

To give herself another minute to decide, she took her time finding a hair clamp. Once she had her long tresses twisted up and secured on the back of her head, she walked to the towel rack, picked out two then hung them on the warmer. Next she lingered over the selection of bath salts.

"What do you think? Lavender, rose or vanilla?" she asked.

"Whichever pleases you. I am not able to smell much."

"Much?" Katie considered what he'd said. "I hadn't thought about that. So you can smell a little?"

"I suspect it is only strong odors that I am able to smell. But even then, they are faint."

"Huh." Katie continued to process the thought even as she absently studied the containers in front of her. Finally she just grabbed one. She checked the temperature of the water, made a quick adjustment then added some of the bath salts.

When she turned around again she couldn't tell if he was amused or waiting to pounce. *Maybe both?*

A quiver ran through her. With trembling legs, she sat on the edge of the tub so she could take off her shoes. She had trouble concentrating on what she was doing, knowing Seamus watched from across the room. And she wasn't bold enough to meet his eye, much less tease or tantalize him.

After her shoes and socks hit the floor she stood and finally looked across at Seamus.

"Have you done this before, Little Katie?" he asked quietly.

"What? Strip in front of a guy?" She shrugged one shoulder in a half apology. "Actually, no, I haven't." When his eyes widened in surprise she quickly added, "I mean, I've been with men before, but we always undressed each other as we were—"

"I understand," he said, cutting her off.

"Sorry."

He smiled. "It's okay. Just relax and pretend that I'm not even here."

"Easy for you to say," she mumbled.

Katie checked the water level to make sure it hadn't gotten too high. She was being foolishly modest. She might be somewhat attractive but based on how open her social schedule typically remained, she didn't attract men by the dozens.

Hoping to distract them both, she said, "You know, the night I met you, I had just taken a long, hot bath."

When Seamus didn't offer any comment she reached for the bottom of her shirt and pulled it off. She tossed it at the hamper then made herself look him in the eye.

"You weren't hanging around in my bathroom where I couldn't see you, were you?"

"Afraid not."

"Good answer." She unbuttoned and unzipped her jeans, pushed them over her hips and down her legs then stepped out of them.

When she bent over to pick up the jeans, Seamus said, "I am sorry I missed the opportunity, however."

The blatant appreciation in his eyes made her feel like one of the most beautiful women on earth. She gave him a smile. "Yes, well, I suppose you're making up for it now, huh?"

"We'll see," he said cryptically.

Katie tossed the jeans on top of her discarded shirt. Gathering her courage, she unhooked her bra then wiggled her shoulders so the straps slid down her arms into her hands. Instead of tossing the pale-pink bra into the pile, she walked up to Seamus and set it on the counter behind him. The cool atmosphere that surrounded him eked onto her bare skin, raising goose bumps and making her nipples harden.

In an effort to up the ante, she slipped her hot-pink lace panties off and left them on the counter with the bra.

Standing that close to him, Katie couldn't miss the desire

burning in his eyes.

Acting braver than she really felt, she pivoted on the ball of her foot and glided to the tub. It was doubtful she had ever made such an effort to ensure she climbed into the bathtub as gracefully as a princess.

As she sank into the steaming water some of the tension in her muscles relaxed. When she was all the way in, she leaned against the back of the tub and studied Seamus.

"Care to join me?"

"As a matter of fact, I would love to. But I believe the only thing that would accomplish would be to cool your water much faster than you'd like."

"That's probably true." Even though she guessed that would be the case, it still disappointed her.

"Besides, the view is better up here," he said with a cheeky grin.

Katie looked down at herself. The waterline bobbed just below her breasts, acting as a pillow for them.

She rolled her eyes but smiled back. "Men."

"What would you do without us?"

"Women would probably eat a lot more chocolate, wear sweatpants more frequently and odds are that neither bras nor pantyhose would have ever been invented," she said matter-of-factly.

"Perhaps."

Seamus' gaze drifted down to the water then all the way down the length of the tub to her toes.

"If I could, I'd take that washcloth," he pointed to the short stack of folded linens on the ledge of the tub, "and make sure every part of you was thoroughly cleaned and inspected."

A shiver ran through Katie's body. God, if only Seamus could do that.

He skimmed his hand through the bubbles that floated on top of her bathwater but his movement didn't disturb a single one. Katie bent her knee, breaking the surface of the water, disturbing those same bubbles.

"So…" She sat up, reached for a washcloth then reclined against the back of the tub again. With a lift of one eyebrow, she asked, "Are you implying that I'm dirty?"

"Not at all." His voice remained calm but his expression turned leery.

Katie twisted the cloth with both hands, forcing most of the water out. "Good. I'd hate for you to have a wrong impression of me."

"Be assured that I have a very high opinion of you."

She picked up the bar of soap and enclosed it in the folds of the washcloth. She rubbed both between her hands, making the cloth bubbly. Slowly she extended one leg up, out of the water, then applied the soapy rag as far as she could reach. She repeated the motions on the other leg.

"You missed a spot."

Katie knew he teased even though his face looked quite serious.

She raised her leg again and pretended to inspect it. "Where?"

"Just there." Seamus touched a place behind her knee then let his finger glide down the back of her thigh.

Goose bumps broke out all over her leg.

She tried to tell herself it had been due to the cold from his ghostly essence and had nothing to do with Seamus. But that was a lie. She wanted Seamus to touch her. She wanted to feel his hands all over her body. She wanted to lie beneath him and feel his body possessing hers.

Like she'd never wanted anyone else before.

It was pointless to imagine herself meeting some fairytale Irish hunk and having a wild affair with him. Every time she tried to conjure up that fantasy, the hunk looked just like Seamus.

Why not indulge her fantasies as far as she could in the time she did have with him?

Katie soaped the rag again and applied it to the spot Seamus had pointed out in slow, easy strokes. She let the suds run down her thigh until they floated onto the surface of the water. "Did I get it that time?"

"I think so. But I imagine the other leg needs some work too."

She propped her foot on the edge of the tub behind Seamus then raised her other leg out of the water. Once again she soaped the rag and pretended to thoroughly yet slowly clean her knee and thigh. When she finished, she hooked that foot over the edge of the tub in front of Seamus, giving him a wide-open yet watery view of her pussy.

"Anything else you think needs inspecting?"

His eyes were instantly drawn to the water. When he raised them again, she couldn't mistake the hunger glittering in the hazy orbs. "I can think of a thing or two."

"I'd hate for something to be left unattended." Katie's pulse sped up. *Where had she picked up a sexy-vixen attitude?*

"Raise your hips up out of the water so I can see."

Her heart thudded heavy in her chest but she did as he said.

Seamus leaned close, putting his head right between her thighs. If he had any she would have been able to feel his breath. He touched her clit with one finger.

The contrast of the cold against her warm skin and the tingles from where their bodies merged sent electric shocks straight to her pussy. Her mouth fell open when she let out a gasp.

Katie shivered as he ran his finger down then around her opening and back up to her clit. She bit her lip as the sensations grew stronger. It was a delicious combination of hot and cold. The barely there, electric touches were more than a tease but less than she needed.

She closed her eyes to better absorb the feelings.

When he plunged a finger into her opening her breath caught in her throat. Her pussy clenched in response but had nothing to grip.

Seamus' strokes quickly became maddening. She wanted more. She wanted him. Inside her.

"Seamus, please," she pleaded. "I need to come."

"Help me get you there. Touch yourself."

Katie didn't need further prompting. She reached between her legs and found the spot that cried out for relief. With just a few strokes her head had rolled back and her hips pumped, seeking what she really wanted.

Seamus continued to touch and stroke her pussy. Their hands merged more than once, adding to the sensations she experienced. Every now and then he would plunge a finger into her opening, sending her spiraling even higher.

Finally she crested. A hoarse cry fell from her lips as her whole body shook with her release. She sank back into the water more relaxed than she had been in weeks.

When she opened her eyes, she found Seamus watching her intently.

"You are beautiful when you come."

A smile spread through her. "No one is pretty when they come. Everyone knows that."

"I disagree," he said.

Katie blushed. "Well, thank you." She looked at Seamus' crotch. He had a very impressive hard-on. "Can I help you with that?" She nodded to his lap.

"I would love for you to help with that, but I suspect that I will have to take care of it later."

"Where's the fun in that?" She cocked her head to the side as she realized could see the wall on the other side of Seamus.

"I—"

Katie sat up in the tub. "Seamus? What's going on? Why can I not see you clearly? It looks like you're fading."

"Damn. I'm sorry, Little Katie. This happens sometimes."

"What happens? What's wrong?" She tried to reach for him but her hand passed through him with only a few mild tingles.

"I have to fade out for a bit and regain my strength." His sounded as if he had moved across the room event though he hadn't moved.

"You mean like falling asleep?"

"A bit."

"But you'll come back?"

He smiled as he reached for her face. "As soon as I can. Hopefully in the morn."

"Okay." Her heart twisted in her chest as she watched Seamus fade away. One more thing that was completely unfair about his situation.

There had to be a way to break that damned curse. If one selfish twit who knew nothing of witchcraft or the paranormal could bring it about, surely she could find a way to reverse it.

It was too bad there wasn't a way to throttle a ghost. If Etain really did haunt someplace in the castle, Katie would love a chance to tell her off. The idea of pushing Etain off the battlements crossed her mind but Katie quickly dismissed it. She could never do that. Besides, it probably wouldn't do anything to a ghost anyway.

Katie didn't know how long she sat in the cooling water. Seamus wasn't going to just reappear so soon and wishing wasn't going to make it happen.

She got out of the tub and grabbed a towel off the warming rack. As she dried off she thought about what she could do to help Seamus. Etain held the key to breaking the curse. She was sure of it. But it was doubtful she could just walk up and ask Etain for the answer.

As Katie stood in front of her closet debating what to put on, it occurred to her that it might be a little too early for bed. She glanced at the bedside table and spotted one of the castle brochures. She had read something about the castle having a library. There were supposed to be current books available for guests to check out and a section on the castle's history. Perhaps she could find some information about Etain.

She pulled a pair of jeans and a sweatshirt out of the closet.

Anything she could learn about Etain would help at this point.

8

SITTING at a large table with of a bunch of dusty, old books, Katie wondered what she had been thinking.

Most of the books were so old she feared handling them. But the librarian said she was welcome to read them. She just couldn't leave the library with them.

Completely understandable.

So far she hadn't been able to find anything more than a passing reference to Etain and the fact that she had been the first wife of Lord Thomas Chichester. Far more information had been recorded about the second wife. Apparently that marriage turned out better and resulted in heirs for the lord.

If Etain really did sleep with that many men she had been fortunate to not have a dozen children. Then again, even back then women could do things to keep from getting pregnant.

Katie wondered if Etain ever caught some nasty itch or virus while hopping from bed to bed. Good thing Seamus never touched her.

Katie shivered in revulsion.

"Ah, there it is," a voice said from just behind Katie's right side. "I'd wondered where the family tome had gone. Was always a favorite of mine."

Without looking up from the page she had been scanning so she didn't lose her place, Katie waved to the pile to her right. "I'm through with those, if what you're looking for is in there."

When she didn't hear a response and no one took a book from the pile she'd indicated, she looked up and over her shoulder.

A thin, elderly man wearing an outfit that looked like something from an Elizabethan play hovered just to her right. His eyes were wide behind his ancient spectacles despite his semitransparent form.

"My dear, were you speaking to me?" the man asked.

She glanced around the room to make sure no one else heard their interaction. It appeared they were alone. She took a deep breath, knowing she had already given herself away by speaking to him.

"I'm afraid so," she said with a tentative smile.

"How is this possible?" he asked as he stepped closer. "I didn't bring forth my form."

"I, uh," Katie hesitated and glanced around again to make sure they really were alone. "I can sometimes see ghosts."

"And hear them too, no doubt."

She nodded as she chewed on her lip.

"Well, that's wonderful, my dear," he said as he sat on the chair at the end of the table.

"It is?"

"Certainly! It's not every day that we have a medium visit us. And it does get rather dull with only a handful of spirits to talk to."

"I'm not a medium."

"But you said you speak to the dead."

"Well, yes, but I'm not a medium. I have just always been able to see ghosts."

"Ah. Born with it, were you?"

"Afraid so," she said dully.

"Oh where are my manners? Please forgive me, my dear. My name is Alastar." He made a half-bow from his seat. "I've been the library guardian for more generations than I can count."

Katie smiled. "It's nice to meet you, Alastar. My name is Katherine."

"You're from the Americas, are you not?"

"Yes."

"On holiday?"

"Of sorts. I'm here to fulfill a request of my late mother."

His ancient eyes seemed to look right into her soul. "And whatever is a lovely young woman like yourself doing buried beneath these," he waved to the pile of books scattered across the table, "crumbling texts instead of out enjoying the nightlife or whatever it is that young people do for fun these days?"

She smiled. "I'm looking for a bit of castle history for a friend."

"Tullamore history? I know more about it than anyone, living or dead. What can I help you find?"

He probably could find it faster than she could ever hope to.

"Do you know anything about a former lady of the castle from the 1700s, named Etain?"

Alastar drew back in surprise. "I do, but what surprises me is that you know of her."

"Why?"

"There is very little recorded about her time here. Her husband had all family records altered so that only a brief mention of her marriage and death were left. The lord, her husband, was quite embarrassed by the ordeal."

"The ordeal?" Katie asked.

"The murder and all of the stories that came with it."

"Ah."

"So you've heard of it."

"I heard that she had been involved in the disappearance and possible murder of a man who worked here."

"That's right." He leaned forward, shifting his weight onto his elbow, and looked at her intently. "But where did you hear of this?"

"From someone who used to do work around the castle," Katie said, trying to keep a blank expression on her face.

He studied her face. "Hmmm. The stories circulating at the time said Etain had an affair with one of the workers. At some point the man tried to break if off with Etain and she, being the jilted lover, killed him."

"That's what the stories said?"

"It is," Alastar said.

"And what do you believe happened?"

"You'll remember that I've been at Tullamore for centuries. I was here before Etain's time."

"So you witnessed it, then?" Hope sprang to life in Katie's heart.

"Not directly."

Hope deflated.

"But I did listen to the charges brought before the lord regarding the man's disappearance as well as the testimony of those involved. And I heard a great deal of the servants talk."

"So how did he die?"

"Supposedly she poisoned him."

"And what of his body? Where was he buried?"

"That is the oddest part." Alastar dropped his voice to a conspiratorial whisper. "The body was never found."

"Not ever?" Katie found herself whispering back.

He shook his head. "Popular rumor said she poisoned him out in the woods and left his body for the wolves."

Katie shivered in revulsion.

"My apologies, my dear. It is a gruesome business."

"You said that was popular rumor. What did the evidence say she did?"

"Some of the kitchen maids testified seeing Lady Etain in the kitchens the day before the man's disappearance, with her maid, cooking something. Needless to say, Lady Etain never darkened the door of the kitchens much less prepared any kind of food so her presence caused quite a stir, and it was well remembered."

"Did they say what she cooked?"

"One of the maids said that Lady Etain had requested a number of unusual herbs be brought to her from the gardens. One or two of those herbs were not grown in the castle gardens and had to be purchased from town."

"I don't suppose a transcript of the testimony was recorded, was it?"

"Actually it was."

Katie perked up. "Where?"

"The lords have always kept journals whenever verdicts had to be rendered. Particularly if those verdicts involved criminal activity and punishment."

"Any way I could see the one about Etain?"

"I'm afraid not. A fire in the late 1700s destroyed a great many of those documents."

Katie's heart sank once again. "Can you think of anything else that might give me clues into what happened to the man Etain supposedly killed?"

Alastar cocked his head. "Her journals might tell you something."

"Her journals?" It was almost too much to hope for.

"Then again, she was quite mad. I've never read them, so they could be full of nonsense."

"Where are they? And would they let me read them?"

"They are considered part of the family books and therefore kept in the family wing. Oddly enough, her journals were not discovered until some time after her death. They believe Lady Etain's maid hid the books, knowing his lordship would have destroyed them."

"So, can I see them?"

"You would have to ask Alanna. She controls who is allowed to see the family pieces."

"Ah. I see. Well, it's worth a chance, right?"

"Depends on what you're hoping to accomplish," he said quietly.

"I hope to be able to give a man back his life."

"That's a noble quest."

"Can you think of anything else that might help?"

"Only Etain herself."

"So her spirit does linger?" Katie asked reluctantly.

He nodded. "And is probably more mad in death than she ever was in life."

"Wonderful," Katie mumbled. "Do you think I could ask her a few questions?"

"You could, but I wouldn't recommend it. The slightest thing sends her into a frenzy. She has frightened more than one guest. Alanna has banished Etain to the battlements for the safety of both guests and staff. There is no telling what she might do if you approached her."

"I see," Katie said. "I suppose that's out then."

"For your own safety, you shouldn't."

She nodded. "I appreciate your help, Alastar. Very much."

"You are more than welcome, my dear. If there is anything else I can do, you can usually find me here." He gestured to the rows of books and tables about the room.

"I will," she said as she stood and gathered the books on the table. "Let me return these to the desk the librarian told me to use."

"Would you do me a quick favor before you go, my dear?"

"If I can."

"There is a book I've been wanting to read for some time, but no one ever leaves it out. I can manage to turn the pages, but getting the book off the shelf and in a comfortable place requires more energy than this old soul can spare some days. Would you mind retrieving it for me and leaving it open on the table?"

"I'd be happy to. Which book did you want?"

"Pride and Prejudice."

Katie smiled approvingly. "That is one book no one should be denied the pleasure of reading."

9

THE next morning, Katie came out of the bathroom to find
Seamus lounging on the bed. She shouldn't be so happy to see him.

"What would you like to see or do today?" he asked as she
made her way across the room.

His eyes scanned her from her head down her bare legs to her
toes and back up again, making Katie flush, despite the fact that
she had a t-shirt and panties on. She stopped at the end of the bed.

"Would you take me to the wisewoman's place? I'd like to meet
her."

His eyes skipped down to her thighs then back to her face
again. "Very well."

"You don't want to know why?"

"Is there a reason you wish to share?"

Katie sighed then sat on the end of the bed and pulled her feet
under her. "There's something you should know."

"If you're needing to tell me something serious, you should put
on a pair of trousers. Otherwise I'm not going to hear everything
you have to say."

"Huh?"

Seamus leaned closer. "You're half naked. I know what you
look like completely naked. I haven't have sex in over three
hundred years. You can't expect me to pay more attention to what
you're saying than to your exposed body."

She rolled her eyes. "All right." She clambered off the bed.
"Hang on a sec." From the closet she grabbed a pair of clean jeans
then stepped into them and pulled them up over her hips. When
she turned around, she found Seamus watching her intently.

The appreciation in his gaze made her stomach flutter.

Somehow she managed to zip and button the jeans then calmly took a seat at the foot of the bed once again.

"Better?" she asked, unable to stop the grin flitting around her lips.

"Depends on how you're looking at it," Seamus mumbled.

"Okay. So I thought I should tell you something before we go." Seamus remained silent and waited for her to continue.

"I may be related to your local wisewoman," Katie blurted, unsure what Seamus might think or how he'd react. Oddly what bothered her more was how much his reaction concerned her.

He showed no reaction for a moment, making Katie even more nervous.

"That would explain the resemblance," he finally said.

"What resemblance?"

"When we met, you reminded me of someone, but I didn't know who. Now that you've said it I see the resemblance."

Katie sat up straighter. "You do?"

Seamus pointed to his own face, making a circling motion around his eye. "It's your eyes, I think."

"Really?" she asked, her voice breaking. "So, it might really be possible?"

He shrugged. "Riona will be able to tell you."

"Well, let's go then." She jumped up and headed to the armoire to finish getting dressed. Butterflies replaced the frisson of heat in her stomach. "Is it very far to her house?"

"The cottage sits on the far side of Tullamore land, so it will be a bit of stroll."

"That's okay, I don't mind the walk."

"It's not the walk that you have to worry about."

Katie stopped digging for socks. "What do I need to worry about?"

"During the day, probably nothing."

"What about at night?"

"There are unusual creatures to be found in the night," he said cryptically.

"Uh huh. So I need to make sure I'm not out walking at night."

"That would be best."

Katie grabbed her raincoat then pulled on her boots. Her room key and cell phone went into her pockets.

"Okay, I'm ready," she said breathlessly.

"Do you want to ask if someone will drive you to the cottage?" Seamus asked as he glided to the entrance.

"No. As long as it's not raining, I'd rather walk." She pulled the suite door closed behind them. "It won't be a problem to get back before dark, will it?"

"Wouldn't that depend on how much the two of you talk?"

Katie chuckled. "I suppose that's true."

They descended the steps and strolled through the lobby in silence. Seamus must have finally understood her need to not draw attention to herself and her gift. As soon as they were out of the hotel and Katie saw no one else about, she asked, "What do you know of the Mac au Bhaird family?"

"Very little."

"You said you knew the local wisewoman a long time ago, right? The one who tried to help you find out what Etain did to you."

"Heloise."

"I assume she was from the same family line?"

"That was my understanding."

"Did she tell you anything of her family?"

"Only when she had to. Remember, these women, while revered by some, were feared by those who did not understand them. They have lived quiet, solitary lives, largely keeping to themselves. Most of what I know of them came from my ma or from listening to talk around Tullamore."

Katie certainly understood the women's reluctance to disclose any gifts they might have. Particularly back when they could have easily been persecuted for being "different".

"Alanna sometimes calls upon Riona for assistance with issues around the castle. I think Riona also supplies one of the gift shops with soaps and perfumes and other stuff women like."

As they talked, Katie realized they were following a path that appeared to run around the formal gardens and skirted the edge of a small forest. She tried to remember what she had seen in the hotel brochure about the layout of the estate. There were cliffs overlooking the beach on the other side of the forested area.

Something about the forest made her think of the Little Red Riding Hood fairy tale. She wondered if the wolf lurked in the shadows, waiting to follow her to grandma's house.

"Nothing is going to jump out of there and grab you," Seamus said. "Not during the day anyway."

He must have noticed her repeated glances at the woods.

"I don't know why but I get the strangest feeling I'm being watched." She quickly added, "And I don't mean by you or in a good way either. I mean the creepy, I'm-not- sure-it's-safe way."

Seamus looked into the dark and eerily quiet woods. "As long as you remain on the trail you'll be fine. I can go take a look if it would make you feel better."

"No, that's okay. If you think it's safe, I'd rather keep moving." It had been sweet of him to offer. "Thank you though."

In order to focus on something else she asked, "Tullamore has ghosts and obviously they have a local witch. More than once you've alluded to other things around the estate. What else can I expect to see in the next couple of weeks? Trolls? Little fairies flitting about?"

"I wouldn't talk about the wee ones." He lowered his voice. "You never know who might be listening."

Katie turned and looked at Seamus in disbelief. Had he implied there might be fairies? Surely he was just teasing. "But no trolls," she asked with a hint of sarcasm.

"I haven't heard of any moving into the area. Alanna would pitch a fit if one did. They're hell on the landscaping."

Katie stopped walking and stared at Seamus. "You must be joking."

He paused and looked back at her. "About trolls being destructive? No, actually, I'm not."

"You're saying trolls are real."

"Certainly."

"You've seen one?"

"Once. Before the curse." He motioned her to keep walking. As soon as she caught up to him, he continued. "When I was returning to Kilmorny, after getting supplies in Stonebriar, I came upon one. He ran a mill and rented rooms to passing travelers. At first glance, you would think him simply a short, ugly man.

"After dinner, I offered to help him move a few bags of grain. As we finished restacking the bags, he tripped over something and his hat fell off. Before he could put it back on, I noticed his ears. They were tall and pointed."

"That doesn't make him a troll," Katie said with a frown.

"He also had a tail. It slipped out before he could right

himself."

"A tail?"

He nodded.

Unsure what to believe, she asked, "What did you do?"

"I turned away and pretended I hadn't seen anything." At her questioning expression he added, "I didn't want to lose a warm, clean and inexpensive place to stay. But I didn't forget."

"I'm sure you didn't."

"It wasn't until some time later that I learned the mill owner had been a troll."

"Wow. You're serious."

"Of course."

Katie fell silent as she absorbed the story. She barely noticed the path they followed and didn't realize they had left the dark forest behind.

Finally Seamus spoke up. "Riona's cottage is just over that hill." He stopped where the path made a sharp turn to the right and pointed across the meadow that lay before them. "We'll have to find our own way from here."

"I thought you said it was safe as long as we stayed on the path. Why are we stepping off?"

"As we passed the forest, that's true. This continues on to Kilmorny, but the way we're going, once we cross through the wards we'll be on protected land."

"Protected? Protected by whom?"

"By the women who have aided and protected this land and the people on it for hundreds of years."

"Riona?"

He nodded. "And those who came before her."

Seamus stepped off the path then turned and waited for her.

Katie hesitated long enough to debate her choices. She shrugged inwardly. In for a penny, in for a pound. As soon as her foot sank into the grass she heard a buzzing in her ears and all the hair on her arms stood on end. The feeling only lasted a few seconds but troubled her.

"Why do I feel like I've fallen down the rabbit hole?" she asked when she reached Seamus.

He looked at the ground around her feet. "The rabbit hole?"

"Alice in Wonderland?"

Seamus' expression remained unchanged.

"It's a book." She waved away the thought. "Never mind. So where are we going?"

"This way."

Katie followed Seamus through the meadow and over one small hill. It was an easy hike despite the damp grass they were marching through. Clouds kept the temperature down, so even after walking what felt like more than a mile, she wasn't sweating.

Finally she saw a small house in the distance. "Is that it?" Katie asked. "That's the cottage."

As they got closer Katie noticed smoke coming from the chimney. A warm fire and a cup of coffee sounded really good.

"Do you think she will be able to tell me more about my mother's family?"

"There is only one way to find out."

A woman came out of the cottage. She watched them for a moment then walked to the gate of the short fence that surrounded the area in front.

"Is that Riona?" Katie asked.

"It is."

Katie's heart beat heavily in her chest.

"Worry not, Little Katie. She will like you."

"I'm not worried."

"You are. I can tell."

Katie looked at Seamus questioningly.

"As soon as you saw Riona, your hands curled and you started fidgeting with the ring on your thumb."

She opened her mouth to deny what he said but realized it was pointless and settled for a noncommittal grunt.

"I'm willing to bet your heart is beating faster too." He looked at her with a mischievous leer. "It's too bad I can't stick my hand under your shirt to find out."

Katie's eyes widened and she stumbled over something. "Ooooh, you are a devil, aren't you?" she asked when she regained her footing.

"Not at all."

"Harrumph."

"It took your mind off meeting Riona, didn't it?"

Katie tried to hold back the smile that played about her lips. "Maybe."

"I bet it did," he teased.

"Even if it did, I wouldn't admit it to you."

They bantered back and forth until they reached the yard.

"Good morning," the woman called out in greeting.

"Good morning. Are you Riona?"

"Some know me by that name."

Katie pasted a smile on her face and approached the gate. Riona was of similar build to herself. Average height, perhaps an inch taller than Katie. Her hair was darker than Katie's with coppery strands. Even though Riona tied it at the back of her neck, Katie could tell it was long and somewhat wavy, like hers.

Katie extended her hand. "My name is Katie Ward, I'm a guest at Tullamore."

Riona hesitated before placing her hand in Katie's.

"I heard about you and wanted to meet you."

When their hands touched, Riona's eyes widened in surprise. She mumbled something in a language Katie didn't understand.

"I'm sorry, but what did you say?" Katie asked.

"You are family. How can this be?" Riona asked as she clasped her other hand over their joined ones.

"Do you know someone by the name of Deirdre Aideen Ward, er, I mean Mac au Bhaird?"

Once again Riona's eyes widened in surprise but then narrowed. "I haven't heard that name in many years. Who is she to you?"

Katie sensed Seamus move closer then noticed Riona's eyes flickered in his direction. She took a deep breath. "She was my mother."

Riona's voice dropped. "Was?"

"She died about three years ago."

"I am very sorry to hear that." Riona released Katie's hand. She unlatched the gate then stepped back, opening it as she moved. "You are welcome in my home, cousin." Her eyes moved to Seamus. "Your spirit guide as well."

10

"ARE you really my cousin?" Katie looked at Seamus. "And can you really see him?" She couldn't decide which surprised her more.

Seamus looked equally surprised.

Riona smiled. "Yes and somewhat. I see a shadowy figure but it is light, not dark."

"Thank you," Seamus mumbled as he followed Katie through the gate.

"Are you able to hear him too?"

"Not clearly."

"Oh." Katie wasn't sure if she was disappointed for Seamus' sake or so she would feel less freakish with her gift. "I feel a little silly introducing someone you can't really see or hear, but this," she gestured to Seamus, "is Seamus MacDonhnaill."

Riona's brow furrowed as if she were trying to recall something. "MacDonhnaill. That is an ancient name."

"He used to live somewhere around here," Katie said.

"I'll have to think about where I've heard it before," Riona said then waved them toward the door of the cottage. "If you've come from the castle then you've had a long walk and must be anxious to sit for a wee bit." She showed them to a cozy den where a fire roared in the fireplace.

There was a short sofa loaded with pillows, a plush armchair and matching ottoman and an ancient wooden rocker. Bookshelves lined one wall. Each shelf had been crammed with books or odd collectibles. A cat slept in a sunny spot beneath one window. The room was feminine and charming and Katie immediately felt at ease.

"Would you like tea or coffee?"

"Coffee would be nice."

"Sit, please. Make yourself comfortable. I'll just be a moment."

Seamus continued to stand as he looked about the room. Katie took a seat on the sofa and almost groaned at how good it felt to get off her feet. She sank into the plump pillows then wondered if she'd be able to get out of the pile.

"You're awfully quiet," Katie said over her shoulder to Seamus.

"I didn't come to visit. I just led the way."

"You know more about these people than me."

"Mostly by reputation. I've only seen Riona in passing a few times. I've never talked with her," he said.

"Well, perhaps you should. Maybe she could help you with the curse."

"Curse?" Riona asked as she returned to the den carrying a tray of teacups and snacks.

Katie looked at Seamus. "Do you mind if I tell her?"

He shrugged. "I don't know what harm it could do."

Katie turned back to Riona. "He said it was fine if I told you."

Riona glanced to where Seamus stood then settled the tray on the ottoman. "Curses are a nasty bit of business." She handed a teacup filled with steaming coffee to Katie. "I have never heard of one going the way it was intended."

Katie took the cup and saucer from Riona and murmured, "Thank you." She inhaled the aroma. It smelled wonderfully rich and spicy. "That's exactly what happened with Seamus."

"He's been cursed then?" Riona stopped arranging things on the tray and looked from Katie to where Seamus stood then back again.

Katie nodded. "The curse is how he became a spirit. Or took on a spirit form, anyway."

Riona studied Seamus' shape. "That explains the difference."

"The difference in what?" Katie asked.

"He looks different than the spirit of someone who has crossed over. I had wondered." Riona selected a couple of crackers and spread some kind of dip on the edge of a plate then handed it to Katie. "He retained his aura but the colors are very watered down. I can barely see it around him."

"Really?" Katie turned to look at Seamus. "Did you know that?"

"I cannot see myself in a mirror, nor can I see auras, so I was unaware of that," Seamus said.

"You can't see yourself in a mirror?" Katie asked in surprise then turned back around to Riona. "I don't know why I didn't think about that."

"It's not surprising that he can't," Riona said. "His spirit form doesn't register to the human eye. He, in a manner of speaking, still has a human eye."

"Ah," Katie said.

"So tell me about this curse," Riona prompted as she and Katie nibbled on the snacks. "Oh I'm sorry, I didn't ask." She looked up at Seamus. "Seamus, would you like something also or can you partake?"

"Thank you, no," Seamus answered.

"He can't eat or drink," Katie explained. "He said thank you for the offer, however."

"I didn't want to be rude," Riona whispered to Katie.

"Of course not," Katie whispered back.

"You two just met. Don't take up your time talking about me and my curse. You need to get to know each other," Seamus pointed out.

"That's very sweet of you, Seamus," Katie said then turned to Riona. "He said we should get to know each other and not worry about his curse."

"That is very nice of him," Riona agreed.

Katie and Riona shared a grin.

"By your accent I would guess that you are from America. What brought you home?" Riona asked.

"Mother's last request."

"What did she ask you to do?"

"She wanted her remains to be brought back to Ireland, Tullamore specifically, and scattered on one of the beaches."

"If you don't mind me asking, why did you wait three years to do this?"

"I didn't know of the request until a few weeks ago. Mother planned this trip before she died. Everything from booking and prepaying the hotel to leaving enough funds in an account to pay for food and transportation. She even picked the days of travel."

"How did you find out about it then?"

"The law firm that handled her will. They managed the account she left and booked the travel as she instructed. Then a couple weeks ago, they called me in and gave me a letter mother had left." Katie pushed a cookie around on her plate. "The letter told me more about my father and why she left home."

"Why did she leave? Ma never knew."

"In a word, me. She was pregnant and she had it in her head that she couldn't stay in Ireland."

"I can't imagine that Ma or even Grandmamma would have criticized her for getting pregnant. Even back then," Riona said.

"According to her letter, it was because of who my father was." Katie's cheeks heated but she wasn't sure why the idea bothered her. "He was a married man. Mom knew there could be no future for them together so she left and never told him about me. She didn't want him to worry or to create bigger problems with his already estranged wife."

"How sad." Riona's voice dropped. "I wonder who he was."

"Mother's letter just said that he was a photographer and somehow related to the Burke family. He had been staying at Tullamore when they met."

Riona frowned. "I remember a man coming here looking for Aunt Deirdre. I was probably about ten at the time. Mom wondered who he was and why he had been so insistent on finding her."

"Did Mom ever write or call anyone?" Katie asked.

"Ma had a letter a few years back. She said it was the first anyone had heard from Deirdre in almost twenty years." Riona scratched the end of her nose. "She told Ma that you would be coming."

Katie tried to force down the lump that always seemed to form when she thought of her mother. Seamus put his hand on her shoulder, making it tingle. She looked up and saw the sympathy on his face. His concern eased some of the tightness in her throat.

"I don't mean to keep dredging up memories that are obviously painful for you, but what happened to Aunt Deirdre? The women in our family usually live long, healthy lives."

"A car accident." Katie swallowed hard. "One day we were planting the seeds in a new garden bed and the next she was gone."

"I'm so sorry," Riona said quietly. "I wish I could have known her."

Seamus rubbed the side of Katie's arm. She wished she could pat his hand to show him she appreciated his comfort. Instead she looked to where he stood behind her and smiled.

"I didn't bring my purse with me, but I have a couple of pictures of Mom back in my room," Katie told Riona.

"I'd love to see them. How long are you staying at Tullamore?" Riona asked.

"Three weeks. I arrived three nights ago."

"Perhaps Ma will return before you leave." Riona tapped her lip. "I'll call her later. She would be disappointed if she missed the chance to meet you."

"Are you an only child also?" Katie asked.

"I'm afraid so." Riona smiled.

"Did Mom have any other sisters or brothers?"

Riona shook her head. "It was just Ma and Aunt Deirdre. From what I've read in the journals, boys are rare in our family."

"Really?"

"Obviously you have your own, er, talents." Riona's gaze darted up to Seamus. "Ma said Aunt Deirdre did too."

Seamus stepped forward. "Tell her I can go out to the gardens if she would rather talk in private."

"Seamus said he could go outside if you want to talk in private."

Riona looked up at Seamus then back at Katie. "Do you trust him with family matters?"

"Yes." She looked at Seamus. They hadn't known each other long but the seeds of trust had taken root in her heart. "Actually I do."

Riona studied Katie for a moment then said, "Then I will as well."

11

THEY shared family stories and the initial unease of meeting someone for the first time wore off. It was nice talking with someone who had similar gifts and could understand the strain and loneliness the gifts created. Riona seemed to have more than one gift however.

"So tell me more about Seamus' curse," Riona prompted.

"I'll tell you what Seamus told me." Katie turned to Seamus. "Stop me if I miss anything."

"All right," he agreed.

"About three hundred years ago, Seamus lived in the area with his family and worked at Tullamore as a woodcarver."

"He's a MacDonhnaill, you said?" Riona asked.

"That's right," Seamus answered. Katie nodded to relay his message.

Riona looked as if she were searching her memory banks. "A very old family. I believe their line died out some time ago."

"I was the last son born to my father," Seamus told them. "My brother had died some years before I was cursed."

Katie repeated what he'd said.

Riona nodded. "Go on."

"Well, apparently, the lord at the time had a wife who was a bit of a floozy." Katie glanced at Seamus as she continued. "Sounds to me like she slept with most of the men in the castle. But when she tried to add Seamus to her list of lovers, he refused her."

Riona's only reaction was a lift of one eyebrow.

"After many attempts and Seamus' continued refusal, Crazy, that's what I've named her," Katie told Riona as an aside, "decided to get a love spell to make him fall in love with her."

80

"Oh dear," Riona mumbled and set her empty teacup on the table.

"Yes, well, it got worse. Crazy then decided the love spell she purchased wouldn't be enough. She broke into the home of the woman she purchased the spell from and stole her spell book."

Riona gasped.

"Crazy combined the ingredients from the love spell with something else. The result," Katie waved her hand in Seamus' direction, "was a man cursed to spirit form."

"Goddess preserve us. I know part of this story." Riona sat up straight on the edge of her seat. "It's in the family journals."

"It is?" Katie asked.

"The spell book being stolen is what stands out. You realize it was an ancestor of ours who made the love spell, don't you? And it was one of our family spell books that was stolen."

"I was afraid you were going to say that." Katie looked at Seamus, afraid of what he might be thinking.

He shrugged. "Tell her about Heloise trying to help me."

"Oh that's right," Katie said, relieved that Seamus wasn't upset about it being her ancestor who provided the original spell. "He told me to tell you about another relative who tried to help him many years ago. Someone named Heloise."

"Really? I'll have to dig her journals out and see if she recorded anything." To Katie, Riona added, "Heloise is our great-grandmother several generations back."

"Oh. Wow." Seamus' true age was hard for her to take in for some reason.

"I told you I was too old for you," he teased.

"Apparently so, if you knew my great-plus-plus-grandmother," Katie groused.

Riona gave Katie a questioning look. Katie waved it away. "Don't ask. He was giving me a hard time, that's all."

Katie stuck her tongue out at Seamus. Laughter rumbled in Seamus' chest and he smiled at her in a way that made the butterflies dance in her tummy.

"Did Heloise have any idea what the other spell was?" Riona asked.

"Not that she mentioned," Seamus said. Katie shook her head to relay his answer.

"Hmmm. Maybe her journals will give us some information."

81

Riona shrugged. "It's possible she had ideas but didn't feel comfortable sharing them with anyone. What else do you know about the spell?"

"I knew nothing at all about the spell," Seamus told them.

"Nothing," Katie repeated.

"I don't mean about the spell itself. I meant about anything anyone would have said to you, something simple. Perhaps even rhyme-like," Riona asked.

Seamus shook his head. Katie mimicked his action.

"Any kind of liquid given to you? Either to drink or something rubbed on you somewhere?"

"Yes!" Katie and Seamus both exclaimed then shared a smile.

"What?" Riona asked.

"Etain had a tankard of something brought to him while he was working. He drank some before he realized it had come from her or that she had poisoned it or whatever." Katie's hands fluttered about as she spoke.

Riona nodded. "I don't suppose you know what was in it, do you?"

"I thought it to be spiced cider at first. I remember smelling herbs as I took a drink."

Katie relayed what Seamus said.

"Any herb in particular?" Riona asked.

"There are very few that I could identify by smell or taste. Mix them in with others, I wouldn't be able to tell one from another." He paced behind the couch.

"No. He didn't know what was in it," Katie said. She hated making him relive so much of the incident. It had to be hard on him.

"It was worth asking." Riona took a bite of her cookie. "What about sweet or sour?"

"Mostly sweet." He moved to a window and looked out. "Seems like it left a bitter taste in my mouth."

"Sweet with a bitter aftertaste," Katie told Riona.

Riona's brow furrowed. "Hmmm. Okay. What happened after you drank whatever she had given you? Did you choke up, vomit, pass out? Or did you just go about your day as usual and later realized that you had turned into a spirit? How long did the change take?"

Katie relayed everything to Riona that Seamus said.

"I remember thinking the tankard tasted odd and asked the maid who'd brought it to me what it was. She said she didn't know, only that Lady Etain had ordered her to bring it to me.

"As soon as I heard that, I knew something foul had been put in the drink. I gave the tankard back to the maid and told her to dump it outside so no one else could drink from it." He looked at the two of them and added, "I honestly thought she had put a poison in the drink in an effort to try and kill me. When my head began to spin and my body felt as if it were on fire, I was sure she was trying to kill me.

"I blacked out several times. A couple of times when I came to, Etain was there asking me things. Telling me I had to tell her I loved her. That if I did, the pain would stop. That everything would be all right."

"Wow," Riona murmured. "That's…" She seemed stunned by the story.

Katie crossed her arms over her chest. "I told him Etain was a nutjob."

"I tend to agree," Riona said softly. "Let me grab a notepad. I want to write this down so I can be sure I have it right when I go through the family records later."

"That's a good idea," Katie exclaimed.

"I'll be right back." Riona stood and walked to the other room.

Katie turned on the sofa and leaned over the back to face Seamus. "Are you all right? I'm sorry you had to relive all of that."

"It's fine." Seamus ran his fingers through a statue sitting on the table next to him. His smile seemed forced. "I can see she wants to help." He rubbed his head. "I'm just not sure there is any help to be had."

"Don't say that," Katie whispered. "There has to be a way to break the curse."

Riona walked back into the room carrying a large book, a notepad and a pencil. She sat the three items on the couch next to Katie.

"What's that?" Katie asked.

"That is Heloise's journal."

"Really?" Katie asked, drawing out the word.

She looked at the book in awe. From the looks of it, the book had been carefully kept. It was aged but not fragile. Rather impressive they had preserved it without climate-controlled technology.

"May I?" Katie asked Riona, pointing to the book.

"Certainly. You're family."

Katie's eyes teared up. "I'm sorry," she mumbled as she blinked back the tears. "It wasn't that long ago that I found myself sitting in the house thinking I had no family. No eccentric aunts or uncles to talk about or annoying cousins to send Christmas cards to. But now I do."

Riona reached across and placed her hand over Katie's. "And I will remind you that you said that after you've been around us a while."

"Deal." Katie smiled.

"Now," Riona said as she grabbed her notepad and pencil, "why don't you take a look at Heloise's journal while I make some notes before I forget what the two of you have just told me. While you're flipping through there, see if you can find any reference to Seamus."

Seamus moved behind Katie and looked over her shoulder. Katie pulled the book onto her lap and gently opened the cover. She kept her movements slow and deliberate so she wouldn't damage anything.

The first entries in the journal looked as if they had been written by someone very young. The handwriting was large and messy. As the pages turned, the entries became more practiced and turned into a feminine script. The topics ranged from the thrill of mixing a first potion to successful gardening tips to descriptions of how difficult situations were handled. Situations like a young mother's child who threw up everything it tried to eat until Heloise created a topical herbal paste that eased the nausea.

"It's amazing to read about herbs being used to help people. She was kind of like a local doctor, wasn't she?" Katie asked.

"I suppose. Back then we didn't have to worry about licenses or lawsuits though," Riona pointed out.

"No, just being burned at the stake or run out of town," Seamus pointed out. "But women like Heloise were also the reason quite a few people survived back then."

"True," Katie said to Seamus then repeated what Seamus had said for Riona.

"Okay. Is anyone else tired of Katie having to be the go-between for me to be able to hear Seamus?" Riona asked.

Katie shrugged. Seamus just looked back and forth between the two women.

"If neither of you mind, I'd like to do a quick spell that should allow me to hear Seamus clearly."

Seamus shook his head and backed away. "No. No spells. I've had enough for a lifetime. The only spell I want on me is the one that will get rid of whatever Etain did."

Katie's heart ached for Seamus. He had every right to be leery. She repeated what he'd said for Riona.

"The spell won't do anything to you, Seamus. It's to me and for me," Riona reassured him. "I can see flickers of you here and there and I hear a muted sound when you're speaking, so I don't believe it would take much to amplify my own natural abilities. However, if you're uncomfortable with me doing it, I won't."

"Perhaps you could do it later, after we leave?" Katie suggested.

"But then she wouldn't know if it worked until she saw us again," Seamus said. He ran a hand through his hair. "If it won't affect me or Katie, then go ahead."

Katie smiled. It was nice to know he was concerned for her as well. And that he was willing to bend. She nodded to Riona that she could proceed.

"Excellent. Give me a moment." Riona scooted around on the couch then closed her eyes.

From the corner of her eye Katie saw Seamus moving away from the couch.

Riona mumbled something in another language that made the hair on Katie's arms stand on end. A gentle breeze wafted through the room then Riona opened her eyes.

"Is that it?" Katie asked.

"That's it." Riona's eyes darted around the room until they landed on Seamus. "Seamus? Say something."

"Double, double, toil and trouble," he said.

Riona smiled. "Fire burn and cauldron bubble."

"It worked?" Katie exclaimed.

Riona nodded. "That's better. He's sounds as if he's talking through a can, but at least I can hear him now."

"Can you see him any better?" Katie asked.

"A little. He's still pretty watery-looking, but at least I can see his expressions now."

Seamus walked back to the couch. Katie couldn't help but grin.

"Excellent. That will be much easier, won't it?" Katie asked Seamus.

"Except now I can't say anything bad about her," Seamus joked.

Katie rolled her eyes. "Oh whatever."

"Okay, so where were we?" Riona asked, returning them to the task at hand.

"We were looking for anything in Heloise's journal about her helping Seamus," Katie reminded her. She flipped open the journal again and Riona scooted in close so she could scan the pages as well.

"Oh here it is," Katie exclaimed. "I found the part where Heloise said she had a ghostly visitor." She looked over her shoulder at Seamus and smiled. "I bet that's you."

"I would hope there wouldn't be a lot of ghosts dropping by," Seamus said.

"Me too," Katie agreed.

"You'd be surprised what drops by here unannounced," Riona muttered.

Katie and Seamus shared a look. Katie wondered if they should ask what Riona referred to then shook her head, figuring she was probably better off not knowing any more than she already did about the spooky things at Tullamore.

Katie skimmed the scribbled entries, looking for anything that might tell them what Heloise knew about Etain. "Apparently it took some convincing to get Heloise to believe what Seamus told her."

"That's true," Seamus said.

"Even more to get her to ask questions at Tullamore," Katie continued.

"Understandable," Riona added.

Katie shrugged one shoulder. "True."

"Why was what I told her so hard to believe?" Seamus asked.

"Because no one wants to think, not even for a second, they might be crazy. And when you're the only one hearing or seeing a spirit, you tend to doubt yourself," Katie pointed out.

Riona nodded her agreement.

"Oh." Seamus' brow furrowed. "I can see where you might have some doubts." He appeared to be dumbfounded.

Katie scanned more of the entries. It was distracting to have to pick through the non-Seamus related ones. When she came to one that talked about Heloise reading Etain's journals, she stopped and read the entry out loud.

"I bet those are the journals that Alastar told me about," Katie said in her excitement.

"Who told you about the journals?" Seamus asked.

"Alastar," Katie said matter-of-factly.

"Who's Alastar?" Seamus' voice dropped an octave or two.

"The library guardian," Katie and Riona said at the same time.

"You mean a ghost?" Seamus asked.

"Yes. Alastar is a spirit," Katie answered.

"Is he the older man that haunts the library?" he asked.

"That's where I ran into him." Katie kept one eye on Seamus' expression. "I don't know if he frequents anywhere else in the castle."

To Katie's relief, Seamus grunted but didn't say anything else.

"Heloise goes on to say she was honored to be allowed access to the family journals but I get the impression she didn't learn much from them." Riona chuckled. "She also says she believes Etain was quite mad."

"Told you," Katie said.

"And I didn't disagree," Seamus told her.

"After reading that, I'm glad I didn't bother asking Alanna for favors so I could read them," Katie said.

"I'm not sure about dismissing them so quickly," Riona said. "I think I'll ask Alanna if I could go through the journals. I'm sure she won't mind."

Katie shrugged one shoulder but didn't look up from the book. "Well, if you know Alanna well enough to ask the favor, it can't hurt. But don't spend a lot of time on them. Even Alastar said they were probably full of nonsense."

"Did Heloise say anything else?" Seamus asked.

"Let's see... Several entries later she says she learned that the granddaughter of Etain's maid still worked at Tullamore."

"Really?" Riona exclaimed. "Did she talk to her?"

Katie nodded as she continued to read. "Yes, she did." She trailed her finger down the page. "The granddaughter told Heloise that she overhead her grandmother telling her mother how guilty she felt for not warning the young man of what Etain planned to do."

"Did she say what Etain did though?" Riona leaned in and looked at the journal.

"No," Katie replied. "The granddaughter said she remembered her grandmother being concerned about what happened after death. She was convinced Etain never left Tullamore, even after being hanged. Supposedly her grandmother swore she smelled Etain's perfume for years after she had died and on occasion heard Etain's voice echoing through the castle."

"That would be enough to make most people a little paranoid," Riona said.

"Not enough to make her leave Tullamore though," Katie observed.

"No, but then again, there aren't many places to work around here," Riona pointed out. "And if the grandmother had been here for some time, I'm sure she would have been reluctant to leave."

"Some people are loyal to the place, not the people they work for," Seamus added.

"True," Katie agreed.

Riona nodded.

"Okay, so nothing very helpful there," Katie said, disappointed.

Katie turned the page of Heloise's journal and found a folded piece of paper stuck into the crease of the journal. It was dirty and faded and looked as if it had been crumpled into a ball then flattened out at some point.

Curious, Katie opened the paper. Riona looked over Katie's shoulder as she read.

"This looks like some kind of spell," Katie pointed out.

"It is…" Riona mumbled.

"It says it's for getting the dead to do your bidding," Katie said.

Riona's brow furrowed and she looked closer. "Actually that looks familiar."

Katie handed the piece of paper to Riona.

"Oh my God. Do you know what this is?" Riona asked as she took the paper from Katie.

Katie shook her head.

"It's a page from one of the family spell books," Riona told them. "One of the first ones."

"But why would Heloise put the page in her journal?" Katie asked.

"What does that scribbled note on the edge there say?" Seamus asked, pointing to one corner of the paper.

Riona angled it into the light. "May God forgive me for keeping my lady's secrets." She looked up at Katie. "The handwriting isn't Heloise's. I bet this is the page that Etain tore out of the family spell book when she supposedly borrowed it. And I'll bet that this spell," she pointed to the spell that had a couple of items circled, "was part of what Etain did."

"Why do you think her maid kept it?" Katie asked.

"Evidence in case I turned up dead?" Seamus suggested.

Katie looked back at Seamus. "Maybe."

Riona nodded. "Very possible." She absently tapped her thumb on her thigh. "I need to read the journals to see what was in the love spell Etain originally purchased. That list of ingredients plus this," she pointed to the missing spell book page, "may give us an idea of what Etain mixed up. The next thing we need to break her curse is her intent behind the spell."

"Her intent?" Katie asked.

"What she wanted to accomplish or what she wanted to gain by using the spell," Riona said.

"We already know that," Katie said.

"We do?" Riona asked.

"Yes. Heloise figured it out and told Seamus. Etain wanted Seamus to fall in love with her. The spell can't be lifted until he finds his one true love."

"Hmmm." Riona tapped the side of her head and appeared to be thinking. "Let me think on this a bit more. Like I said, I want to read through a few of the family journals and see if I can't piece something together. Mother has a close circle of friends that we can call on for information also. Between them, they have centuries of knowledge at their fingertips."

Katie looked at Seamus. "See? There's a chance we can figure this out."

He gave her a tight-lipped smile. "Maybe." He shrugged. "I hesitate to get my hopes up. I've been living with this for so long I don't remember what it feels like to be human."

Katie and Riona looked at each other.

"I don't want your pity. What's done is done and it was no fault of yours," Seamus said. "But I'll thank you for learning everything you can before all traces of what Etain did are gone."

Determination set up camp in Katie's heart. If there was a way to break the curse, she would find it. Even if it meant talking to every ghost in the castle.

With a glance out the window Seamus added, "We should probably be heading back to the castle. I don't want you walking back after dark."

"Don't be silly," Riona waved his concerns away. "Stay for supper. I can drive you back later."

Katie smiled and Seamus seemed to be pacified by her offer. "As long as we're not interrupting your day, I'd love to stay and have supper."

"Ma is gone and I have the cottage to myself. I'd enjoy the company as well. Besides, you just got here. You can't leave until you've told me about the States."

"As long as you tell me more about your mom and what you remember of Grandmother. Grandfather too, if he was around."

"I'd be happy to," Riona assured her.

"If you're in Riona's care," Seamus shared a look with Riona, "then I'll make my way back to the castle and let you two have family time."

"I will see to her safe return," Riona assured him.

"Okay, guys, I'm not a child that has to be looked after." Katie was partly flattered he cared but also annoyed that he thought she needed a keeper.

Seamus floated around and knelt in front of Katie. "I know you're not a child, but there are things at Tullamore that really do go bump in the night. Things you know nothing of and hopefully never will." He looked to Riona. "I strongly suspect that I don't know half of them."

Riona looked away.

"I want to make sure you aren't wandering around on your own after dark."

Pacified, Katie agreed. "All right. Quit your worrying. I'll be fine." She reached out and patted him on the cheek. Or tried to anyway. "Riona can drive me back later. Go recharge your batteries or whatever you do in your spare time."

He stood and floated toward the door.

Katie called out. "But I don't mean for you to go checking out any new guests!"

She didn't think it was possible for a ghost to blush but she would have sworn Seamus did as he disappeared through the wall.

12

RIONA dropped Katie at the castle right after dinner because Riona received a call asking for help with a difficult birth and she needed to pick up a couple of things on the way.

The afternoon had been wonderful. Riona had shared their family history and Katie looked forward to meeting her aunt. Riona also offered to give Katie a blessing spell for when she scattered her mother's ashes.

Knowing she did have family eased some of the pain her mother's death had left. Even if the Mac au Bhaird line turned out to be more quirky than the Simpsons, they would be forever connected.

Since it was still early, Katie headed to her room to see if Seamus lurked about somewhere. She found him lounging on the bed, watching TV.

"What are you watching?" she asked as she walked in.

Seamus frowned at the TV. "I'm not sure. I managed to turn the thing on but can't change the show. This seems to be about the reproductive system of some kind of underwater creature."

"How fascinating. Are you enthralled with the sea urchins or would you rather ramble about the castle with me?"

He hopped off the bed. "Actually I thought of something that you might find interesting."

"Oh?"

"How do you feel about expanding your boundaries again?"

"How far are you planning on expanding them?"

"That would be entirely up to you. Come on, I'll show you."

Katie followed Seamus through the castle then down several flights of stairs.

When she realized she had no idea where they were, she asked, "Where are we going?" Her voice echoed off the stone surrounding them on the floor, walls and ceiling.

"I thought you might want to see the dungeon," Seamus told her.

"Dungeons? Like where they used to keep prisoners?"

"Prisoners or those deemed insane. Later they used it for storage."

"What do they use it for now?"

The half-grin on Seamus' face made Katie wonder what he was up to. "You'll see," he said mysteriously.

Katie could well imagine what this area must have been like three hundred years earlier—cold, dark, damp and probably smelly. At least now there were electric lights along the walls and drains in the floor. Granted, the lights had been made to look like candles, including the flickering flame. They didn't provide a lot of light, but it had to be better than it had been four hundred years earlier.

When they came to the end of the hall, Seamus directed her to the right, down a short passage then around another corner. There, she was surprised to find a large desk, manned by a voluptuous woman dressed in some sort of gothic costume.

"Good evening. Welcome to the Dungeon. How may I assist you?" the woman asked.

"Er...?" Katie looked at Seamus, unsure what she needed to say.

"Tell her that Vlad sent you and that you're only viewing this evening," Seamus instructed.

Katie repeated what Seamus had told her.

"Very well." From one of the desk drawers the woman took something but kept it hidden in her hand. She stood and stepped to the end of her desk. "If you will follow me."

Katie nodded, unsure what else she could say. Once the woman had turned away she shot a look at Seamus, conveying her unease with the situation.

The woman led the way to an inconspicuous doorway. She passed a security card through the electronic lock then opened the door. After she stepped through she held the door open for Katie.

She stepped into an even darker hallway than the one they'd just followed. This one had been carpeted at least and had small lights along the floor on both sides. The lights made the area look a bit like an airport runway.

The woman led the way to the end of the hall then unlocked another door. When Katie stepped through this doorway she found a large open room with several groupings of couches and chairs and a manned bar at the far end. Around the perimeter of the room were multiple passageways.

Fake torches were scattered about the room making it brighter than the hallway, but not overly so.

"You will need to wear this necklace," the woman dangled a silver chain from her finger, "and keep it visible as long as you are within the Dungeon walls. It signifies you are not available for play. If anyone approaches you, simply notify one of the attendants."

Katie slipped the thin, dog tag-like chain over her head. A pendant stamped with a dragon or some kind of winged mythological creature dangled at the end of the chain.

"As a guest of Vlad, you may not approach anyone or engage in any form of play. Viewing is permitted in any of the rooms with an open door but do not attempt to enter closed rooms."

"Okay." That seemed to be the most appropriate answer, even though she had no idea what she had really agreed to. As soon as they were alone again, she would be asking Seamus though.

"Do you have any questions?"

"Um, no, not right now."

"An attendant will always be available to serve you."

"Okay. Thank you."

The woman bowed her head then backed away.

Katie took a moment to memorize the door they had come through in case she needed to find it again. From the corner of her mouth she whispered to Seamus, "What the hell have you gotten me into?"

"Just exploring your darker side."

She walked along the outer edge of the large, central room, looking at the furnishings and the people milling about. "What dark side? I'm not aware that I have one."

"Everyone does. Some are just darker than others," Seamus replied. "I'm curious about yours."

"I suspect you're going to be disappointed."

"I doubt it, Little Katie."

Katie faced him. Even with the lower lighting she could see the sincerity and even a touch of admiration in his expression.

Heat warmed her cheeks. "Thank you." She continued her stroll along the perimeter. When she passed one of the doorways she slowed her pace and looked down the darkened passage.

She could hear voices but not well enough to know what they were saying. A crack echoed in the small area, making her jump. Her gaze flew to Seamus. "What was that?"

"What did it sound like?" he asked.

"A whip," she whispered harshly.

"It probably was."

"Seriously?" Her voice squeaked.

"Hard to say. I'd have to look to be sure."

"I'd say that was a very noticeable sound, wouldn't you?" she asked, somewhat offended.

"Normally, yes, but that sound could have also been a leather-encased hand making contact with a bare arse."

Katie's mouth fell open. She blinked to clear the image from her mind. "What?"

"It's very possible down here."

She put one hand on her hip and held up the other one in a "stop" gesture. "Okay. Where exactly is here?"

"The Dungeon," he said without inflection.

"And what exactly is the Dungeon?"

He smiled that smile that made Katie think he knew something she probably needed to know.

"It's a place for people with similar interests to get together in a safe environment."

Katie had the feeling there was more to what he was telling her.

"The woman who led us in here said something about engaging in play. What did she mean by play?" she asked.

"She meant sexual play."

"Sex?" Her eyes nearly bugged out of her head.

"No. Sexual play."

"There's a difference?" she asked.

"In here? Absolutely."

"I'm still confused," Katie admitted.

With a jerk of his head, he said, "Come on. It'll be easier to show you than to explain."

"I think a drink is in order first," she said.

"As you wish."

Katie found the bar and ordered her favorite mixed drink. The familiar warmth in her stomach helped settle her nerves. She was a little out of her element and had no idea what to expect. The only thing keeping her from running out of the room was the necklace the woman said would keep anyone from approaching her.

"Are you okay?" Seamus asked.

"Um, yeah. I think."

"You don't have to stay if you're not comfortable. But I promise you are perfectly safe here. They do not tolerate harassment of guests or violation of any rules."

She took a deep breath. "Okay."

"If you get uncomfortable, just tell me and I will show you the fastest way out."

"Thanks," she said with a smile. "That helps."

"Come. There's something I think you'll find interesting."

Seamus led her to one of the hallways on the far side of the room. She passed a few couples but no one stopped her or asked what she was doing there. She doubted anyone even noticed her.

Thank God.

The warmth from her drink spread and helped her relax.

"We're going to start with something easy," Seamus said as he stopped just before they reached an open door.

"All right." She smiled, touched that he sensed her unease.

"Most of the rooms in this part of the Dungeon are set up for some kind of bondage."

"You mean where people tie each other up?"

"That's right."

She shrugged. "I've heard of people doing that. I even had a couple of friends in college who talked about doing it with boyfriends. That shouldn't be too bad."

"Keep in mind, you can take anything to an extreme."

"True." She made shooing motions at Seamus. "So, come on already. Let's see what they've got around here."

He stepped to the side. "How about if I follow you, then?"

She took one step then paused. "It's really okay to watch these people doing whatever they're doing?"

"They wouldn't be here with the door open if they didn't want someone to watch," he reassured her.

"Good point."

Katie glanced into a couple of rooms as they passed. Just being nosy, she told herself. She saw a wide variety of tools being used and people being put into all kinds of positions. Some were a little bit scary.

Finally one of the rooms induced her to stop.

The room had been painted crimson-red and sparsely furnished with black lacquer cabinets and chairs. From the center of the room a swing made of narrow straps had been suspended from the ceiling.

A voluptuous, dark-headed woman reclined in the swing. She wore nothing except a bright-red satin blindfold across her eyes. Each of her limbs had been secured in the swing by zebra-striped fur cuffs.

The woman had a male partner but instead of doling out some kind of punishment, he skimmed a peacock feather across the woman's breasts and belly. If the smile on the woman's face and her squirming were any indication, she was a bit ticklish.

The man walked to the cabinet on the side of the room and set the feather on the top. He reached into a bucket that had been stored inside the cabinet and pulled something out. Katie couldn't tell what he held right away, but as soon as he touched the woman's nipple with it, she realized it was a piece of ice. The trail of melted water glistened on the woman's skin.

The woman sucked in a breath when he ran the ice over the other nipple then let a few drops of water fall onto her chest. With the ice still in his hand, the man moved around to the front and stood between her legs.

The scene enthralled Katie. Watching a couple engaged in some kind of sexual activity was erotic enough, but for some reason, Katie sensed many of the sensations the woman had to be feeling. The fur cuffs around her wrists. The cold of the ice. The rough texture of her lover's hand on her thigh.

Katie's own nipples beaded into hard pebbles inside her bra and her breasts ached to be touched. A tremor rippled through her body as she imagined what it must feel like to be bound, completely naked, while her partner controlled what sensations she experienced. All while incapable of seeing what might happen next.

The anticipation was probably delicious.

Lost in her haze of sensual overload, Katie wondered what Seamus must be thinking. When she looked at him, she found him watching her instead of the couple or the swing.

Their eyes met. She couldn't mistake the longing she saw there.

A frisson of need spiraled through her and set her soul on fire. She swallowed. Hard. Then forced herself to turn back to the couple in the room and forget about the things she and Seamus couldn't do together.

If she dwelled on the things she wanted with Seamus, she would drive herself mad.

Even though she faced the room, her mind didn't register what she was seeing for a moment. The man had knelt between the woman's legs, and now played with her pussy. Did he still have a piece of ice in his hand though?

The woman squirmed in the swing, but with nothing to leverage against, she couldn't move. She was pretty much at her partner's mercy. That didn't necessarily seem to a bad position to be in.

The ice probably made a startling contrast against the heat of the woman's crotch. As Katie contemplated the allure of the situation, she watched the woman arch her back. "Oooo," the woman cooed.

Both of the man's hands roamed across the woman's belly and thigh. Without the ice. Nothing had fallen to the floor. Had he pushed the piece into the woman's pussy?

Suddenly the man grabbed the woman by her hips and buried his face in her crotch. The woman's mouth fell open and she sucked in a loud gulp of air then moaned. Even though Katie could only see the back of the man's head, it looked, and sounded, as if he gave his attentions rather enthusiastically.

"I've heard that if you do the alphabet with your tongue, it provides the woman a wide variety of sensations," Seamus said as he floated next to Katie and watched the couple.

"The alphabet?" Katie asked then forced herself to blink away the image his comment created in her mind.

"I haven't been able to test that theory myself, but I could see where it might work."

"I doubt that's what he's doing," Katie said with a tilt of her head in the direction of the couple.

"If he is, those are some of the sloppiest letters I've ever seen."

Katie had to slap a hand over her mouth to keep from laughing out loud. She certainly didn't want to interrupt the couple or make them think she was laughing at them. When she regained control, she whispered, "Stop that. You're going to make me embarrass myself."

"Before I interrupted, you seemed to be enjoying yourself. What about this," he pointed to the couple in the swing, "appeals to you where the previous rooms or couples didn't?" Seamus asked.

Keeping her voice low, she admitted, "I wondered the same thing. In most of the other rooms, the woman had been bound and the man stood in charge."

"True," he agreed.

"I suppose the most obvious difference is the punishment versus teasing or tantalizing."

"So being tied up doesn't bother you then." It sounded as if he had made a statement more than asked a question.

"No," she drew out the O. "The idea of being tied up by someone I trust is not offensive. I wouldn't do something like that with just anyone though. Certainly not a stranger."

"So if you had a longtime lover or husband, would the idea of being subjected to his every whim turn you on?"

Katie's cheeks warmed rapidly. "Yes, a little."

"Does anything else about what you've seen in here," Seamus pointed to the couple in the room, "appeal to you?"

"The swing," she said without hesitation.

Seamus looked back at the couple as if he hadn't even noticed what the woman sat on. "You like the swing? What about it?"

Katie motioned for him to step away from the doorway with her. Even though she kept her voice low she didn't want to disturb the couple.

"There are a couple of interesting things about the swing."

Seamus nodded for her to continue.

"First, the positioning it puts the woman into. It looks as if her lover has access to pretty much every part of her. And it doesn't look uncomfortable. Second, the furry cuffs." Even though they stood in the hallway, she could still see the couple and the swing. "Seems to me those would add a sensation on her skin and yet that is what is binding her too."

"You're probably right."

"The other thing is…" She bit her lip, wondering if she was telling him too much.

"Go on," Seamus encouraged her.

"Well, I just got to thinking that having sex in the swing would probably be a unique feeling. Kind of like floating in the water.

And the guy would be able to control the motion a lot better, I should think."

When Katie looked up at Seamus, he had a pained expression on his face.

"Did I say something wrong? Too much information?" She probably shouldn't have told him everything.

"No," he reassured her. "You didn't say anything wrong. I want to know what you think." He ran his hand through his hair. "I just, uh… I had a vision of what I would do to you if I had even five minutes with you on that swing."

Not only did that vision creep into her head but she saw the raw desire in his eyes. Katie's pussy clenched in response and her panties dampened.

A sound behind her alerted her that another couple headed in their direction. Not wanting anyone to think she was talking to herself, she motioned Seamus to follow her. As they made their way to the main salon, she didn't even glance in the other doorways. Her senses were already on overload.

Once they were back in the salon, she debated getting another drink. With all the ideas and visions spinning around in her head, alcohol would probably be best taken in low doses. Otherwise she might really end up telling Seamus something she shouldn't.

Katie found an unoccupied pair of chairs that were tucked into a shadowed corner of the salon. Before she could even take a seat, one of the highly efficient Dungeon staff stopped to ask if she needed anything, but Katie shook her head and waved her on.

"What do you think of the Dungeon so far?" Seamus asked as he settled into the other chair.

"Let me put it this way. Even if I found a club similar to the Dungeon back home, I don't see myself hanging out in a place like this."

"I wouldn't expect you to. I meant, what do you think about the things you've seen?"

"Ah. Well, it's been interesting. And, yes, I admit to being turned-on by a few things, but it's a lot to take in."

"I'm sure it is if you've never been around this lifestyle," he agreed.

"I assume you found out about this place as a result of your problem?"

His eyebrow raised in question. "My problem?"

"Your bad habit of spying on people."

He chuckled. "You say problem. I say form of amusement."

"Harrumph." Katie turned her head to visually follow an odd-looking couple as they passed through the salon. The woman had to be close to six foot tall. She had a stocky build and long blonde hair. Katie couldn't help thinking of the Viking wife in that cartoon, Hägar the Horrible. The man who accompanied the Viking woman however was several inches shorter and skinny as a rail. The woman probably outweighed him by more than a hundred pounds.

Her mind came to a screeching halt as she wondered what the two of them would be doing in the one of the rooms.

"That does put me in mind of something," Katie said.

"In mind of what?" Seamus asked.

"Why haven't I seen any men getting tied up by a woman?"

"Because they tend to stay in that hallway." He pointed across the salon in the opposite direction.

"Oh." Katie perked up. "What else do they do over there?"

"I'm not certain. I haven't spent much time there."

"Why not? Don't like the idea of being tied up?" she teased.

"Not really." He leveled his gaze on her. "Although, like you, with the right woman, I would do it if she wanted."

Katie fought to control a shudder that rippled through her when she thought of Seamus tied up, maybe even blindfolded, and hers to do with as she pleased. More heat pooled between her legs.

"Does that interest you, Little Katie?"

Seamus' voice sounded like a sexy purr. Goose bumps popped up on her arms.

"Maybe," she said coyly.

"I think it does," he said and leaned closer. "Your breathing changed and even in this light I can see that you've turned pink. Your panties are probably wet too."

Katie squirmed in her seat. She looked across the salon to avoid looking him in the eye. He just saw too damn much of what she was thinking.

She blinked in surprise when she spotted a familiar face. "Isn't that the woman we saw a few days ago making out with the ghost in the lobby?" Katie tried to discreetly point the woman out to Seamus. Now that Katie could see all of her, she wished she hadn't. The woman wore a formfitting knit dress that showed all her curves to her advantage.

Katie felt seriously underdressed in her jeans and sweater.

"I believe it is," Seamus agreed. "Didn't you say you ran into her in the lift?"

"Yeah. Shanna was her name, I think. She said she had been looking for her ghost boyfriend, but I didn't want to tell her I could see him."

When Shanna turned to navigate around a couch, Katie saw the bare-chested ghost the woman had been making out with walking beside her. "Apparently she found him. I wonder what they're doing down here."

Seamus turned to look at Katie, one eyebrow raised in question. "I should think they are down here for the same reason we are."

"Well, yeah. I mean…" Katie rolled her eyes. "Oh shut up. I know it's a stupid question."

Seamus chuckled. "So long as you know it too."

"Whatever," she said as she folded her arms across her chest then pretended to pout.

Katie kept an eye on the ghost couple, just out of curiosity. "They're going the way we came in." She smiled at Seamus. "Think they're into something heavier than the swing?"

"I'm not sure," Seamus said, though he looked distracted. He also watched the ghost couple. When the couple disappeared from their sight Seamus hopped up and said, "I'll be right back. Don't go anywhere without me."

He didn't give her a chance to agree or disagree, just floated to the same hallway the ghost couple had taken. She had been kidding when she said she wondered what the other couple would be doing. Why did Seamus take it so seriously?

While he was gone, Katie used the time to think about what she had seen. Once she got over her perception of "spying" on people, it was a bit like watching highly erotic porn. Thankfully without the moaning and groaning and fake orgasms. But it had a stronger impact because these were real people, not paid actors.

Seamus returned with a frown on his face.

"What's wrong?" Katie asked.

"They left."

"Shanna and her friend? Were they just passing through?"

"Looks like it," he said with a shrug.

"How strange."

"I wanted to stop them and ask how they are able to..." He made a gesture with his hand that Katie didn't understand. "How they can touch each other if he's a ghost."

"Oh." The implication sank into Katie's brain. "Oh!"

"Yeah."

"Wouldn't that be..." Her thoughts scattered.

Seamus pressed his lips together and nodded briskly.

Katie's face heated and a knot of tension built inside her. Perhaps she should go for another drink. She opted for distraction instead. "Okay, how about another room full of kinky stuff?"

Perhaps that wasn't the best choice for distraction but her choices were limited at the moment.

Seamus chuckled, easing the tension that had built between them. "Why not?"

Katie stood and looked at the different hallways. "You said that one," she pointed at one hallway entrance, "had all the women in charge, right?"

"Yes," he answered slowly, cautiously.

"Okay. Let's go," she said then marched in that direction before she lost her nerve.

Surprisingly there were several couples lingering in this hallway. More than the last one to be sure.

The first room they passed with an open door had a woman dressed in black latex from head to toe. Including a pair of boots that looked as if they could hurt both the wearer and the person she was with. She held a mean-looking whip over the man kneeling on the ground in front of her.

The man wore some kind of open-cheek briefs and had bowed so low his forehead probably rested on the ground.

Katie didn't stay long enough to find out what the woman planned to do with the whip. She moved farther down the hallway without even looking at Seamus to see if he had enjoyed the scene. That would be more than she could handle.

As she walked and scanned the rooms, it occurred to Katie that there were more closed doors in this hallway than the others. But there were windows installed in the wall next to the door of some rooms. A shade had been installed but several were open.

She came to an open room fairly quickly but had to look around the shoulders of another couple to see what was going on. She didn't intend to stay and watch while someone else viewed, but she was curious to know if she'd want to come back if the viewing couple moved on.

Instead of a woman, a drop-dead gorgeous specimen of a man controlled the room. Since he only wore a pair of black leather pants and they fit him like a second skin, she could see almost every detail of his body. The tall, tanned, broad-shouldered Adonis had muscles stacked on top of muscles. Katie was disappointed to see his dark hair had been clipped short. The way he stood with his arms folded across his bare chest as he watched the two women in the room do his bidding, made Katie think he had served in some branch of the military.

The women were both rather pretty but contrasted each other in looks. Neither of them wore more than their panties.

The couple standing in front of Katie moved out of the way, leaving Katie standing there seemingly alone.

The man in the room turned and looked at Katie. His eyes scanned her from head to toe, lingering on her necklace for just a moment.

"You're welcome to join us, if you like."

His comment, although she sensed it had been directed at her, startled her enough that she turned her to see if someone had walked up behind her without her knowing. All she found was Seamus' scowling face.

She faced the man in the room again. "Oh, uh, thank you, but no." Katie tried to smile but it probably looked more like a grimace.

The relief on the women's faces spoke volumes.

Katie backed away and headed to a different room.

"He needs to be reported," Seamus mumbled as they walked.

"Who? The guy in the last room?"

"He wasn't supposed to approach you. You're considered a special guest and under Vlad's protection."

"Don't worry about it. Yes, it made me uncomfortable, but it's not as if he dragged me into the room or anything." Katie shrugged. "I told him no. End of story."

"I don't like it."

Katie stopped walking and turned to Seamus. She studied his expression. The incident obviously bothered him. "Thank you for worrying about me. But despite the newness of all of this," she gestured to the rooms in general, "I honestly don't feel unsafe. Out of my element, for sure. But not unsafe."

He folded his arms across his chest and grunted.

Katie realized even though Seamus wasn't quite as muscled up as Mr. Leather Pants, she preferred Seamus' naturally masculine look over what was probably steroid induced. Not that Seamus didn't have well-defined muscles. He certainly did. And she wished she could lick every single one of them. There was a difference though that she appreciated.

If only he hadn't been changed into spirit form.

"Why are you looking at me that way?" Seamus asked.

"What way?"

"I'm not sure. It's an odd expression on your face."

Katie glanced at the people walking around them. "We better move along." She mumbled, thankful to have an excuse to not delve into what she had been thinking.

The next room they came to appeared to be what she had been looking for. However, instead of an open door the window covered by slated blinds. The blinds were still open but Katie suspected they could be closed easily. In the center of the room a blindfolded man sat in an armless chair with his arms drawn behind his back. The woman in the room with him wore a short black chemise but no shoes.

She stood behind the man, running her hands over his shoulders and down his arms. Every so often she would lean close and whisper in his ear. Then she moved around to the front of the man and sat across his lap.

The woman's lips were moving as she unbuttoned his blue dress shirt. When the man didn't embrace the woman or even run his hands up her bare legs, Katie realized his hands must be bound behind him.

What a delicious thought. Not only could the woman touch him wherever and however she wanted but she didn't have to worry about how she looked to her partner. If she had pimple on her butt he wouldn't see it. She could concentrate on him and his pleasure.

How liberating!

As she watched the couple Katie realized how much more their interaction turned her on than what she had seen in any of the previous rooms. Her skin had become rather sensitive and every time Seamus floated close, the tingles where they touched were more intense and quickly spread to other parts of her body.

The desire to throw Seamus on the floor and lick him all over threatened to override her good sense. Again. She really needed to control herself.

"Something about this one attracts you," Seamus said.

"Why do you say that?" Katie tried to sound casual but doubted she achieved it.

"You're pink again. And you haven't moved since you looked into the room."

She glanced at Seamus with a sheepish grin. "Yeah, so?"

"Not so much an accusation as it is an observation. But I would like to know what it is that you like so well in this room."

Katie tucked a loose strand of hair behind her ear. "I think it's the couple's interaction with each other more than anything. It's a gentler scene. Not so much about pleasure or pain, but rather about caring for the partner and the partner's wants or needs." She shrugged. "That probably sounds cheesy but that's how it looks to me."

Seamus examined the couple in the room then nodded. "I agree. That does seem to be the way they are interacting." He studied Katie for a moment. "And I could see the appeal of it for you."

"You don't think it's appealing?"

"I didn't say that."

"Oh, so is it because the man is the one tied up?" Katie asked.

"No, I didn't say that either."

"So you do like the idea of the guy getting tied up," she pressed.

"I suppose that's fine."

"What if it were you who had been tied up?"

"I don't know. Maybe." Seamus looked away, obviously uncomfortable with the conversation.

"Maybe? You wouldn't want to have someone trying their damnedest to please you and you didn't have to do anything except sit there and take it?"

"If you're offering to be the one to do it, God yes!"

Katie's jaw fell open. The ferocity of the desire in his eye left her stunned. Images rolled through her head of what she could do to Seamus if she had him all to herself, in the flesh, and turned her insides to liquid heat.

She wanted this man more than any other. Something told her they would be very good together. Why did he have to be spirit-bound instead of corporeal?

Sometimes things happen for a reason.

Oh Lord. Now she was hearing her mother's voice in her head. While she was in a sex palace too! This really couldn't get any weirder.

"Are you okay, Katie?" Seamus' brows were drawn into a frown. Concern etched his features.

"Yes. I'm fine." She shook off her thoughts of both Seamus and her mother. "Really," she added when Seamus didn't look as if he believed her. "But I think I've about had enough of the Dungeon for one night."

"As you wish. But there is one more thing I'm interested in getting your reaction to."

"My reaction to what?" she asked hesitantly.

"Come. I'll show you."

Seamus led the way to the end of the hallway then turned a corner into a different area. Katie couldn't put her finger on what made this area different. The paint scheme might have been lighter or perhaps the furnishings a bit more ornate. But unlike the previous hallways, all the doors were open here.

Katie glanced into each of the doorways they passed. There were certainly more people in this area. More people circulating from doorway to doorway and more milling about inside the rooms.

Finally she came to a door where the couple inside was engrossed in each other. Despite their physical differences, they were an attractive couple together. She was a petite Asian woman with short dark hair. He was a tall, lanky man with fair skin and bright-red hair.

Once the man had divested the woman of her dress, she pushed him back until his knees met the edge of the bed then she leaped into his arms, making them both tumble onto the mattress. Their laughter touched a place inside Katie.

That was what sex was supposed to be. Two people, enjoying each other, forming a bond. And it should always be fun. Even at its most climatic or highest intensity, both partners should want the connection and should feel good in the end.

Katie looked over at Seamus. He watched the couple but must have sensed her regard. When he looked in Katie's direction, a smiled hovered about his lips.

Her heart fluttered. She enjoyed being able to share an experience like this with him. They might not have known each other long but she was unusually comfortable with Seamus. She returned his smile then went back to watching the couple in the room.

As the couple got more into their play, Katie realized she was waiting for something big to happen. All the other rooms had an element that made the interaction unusual. The swing, a little bondage, some something that added to the sex. She wondered what it would be here.

Her question was soon answered. Just as she began to relax and enjoy the scene, another couple entered the room. They stopped not far inside the doorway.

"May we join you?" the new man asked the couple who were already in the room.

Katie's face probably registered her surprise. Although why anything she saw in the Dungeon surprised her she didn't know.

The Asian woman looked over her shoulder at the new pair then back at her partner. They exchanged a look or some silent communication then she smiled and answered, "Certainly."

The new couple entered the room and sat on the bed.

Katie was so stunned she didn't pay attention to what they were saying to each other. Her gaze shot to Seamus. He watched her intently.

From the corner of her mouth she whispered, "Are they really going to…" She made a slight gesture with her hand to show she referred to all four of the people in the room.

"It would appear they are."

Katie snapped her mouth shut and turned her attention to the group. Her cheeks burned and her discomfort skyrocketed. She had trouble imagining herself with others while being intimate with her lover or partner.

Both couples adapted quickly to their introduction. Katie was more surprised to see the original couple's obvious affection for each other didn't diminish just because there were two more bodies.

Instead of just pairing up with a new partner, the couples merged. Everyone touched everyone else and arms and legs were tangled and intertwined in what Katie thought resembled an adult game of Twister.

"What are you thinking, Little Katie?" Seamus asked.

"Honestly? I think my brain has seized," Katie whispered.

Seamus chuckled. "Come on. I think you've had enough for one day."

She nodded mutely and let him lead her away.

13

INSTEAD of going back the way they came in, Seamus led Katie around a different path. After a couple more turns she recognized the hallway as the first one they viewed.

Katie slowed her pace so she could take another look at the room with the swing. This time it was vacant. "That swing is really...um, interesting." She chewed on her fingernail as she imagined its different uses. Hmmm… *But where could I buy one?*

If she ever got seriously involved with someone who liked that kind of thing, that is.

"Are you using the room?"

Katie found a young couple behind her. The girl looked hopeful.

"Oh, no, I'm not." She stepped out of the doorway. "Go right ahead."

"The swing is really cool, isn't it?" the girl asked enthusiastically. "I just love it. I told David we need to get one for our place." She squeezed her partner's arm and grinned at him.

He, presumably David, turned pink and shuffled his feet.

"Well, you two enjoy yourselves," Katie said.

"Thanks. You too!" the girl said.

Katie smiled at Seamus as they left the young couple to their play.

"Guess you're not the only one who has an appreciation for the swing," he said.

"Guess not," Katie mumbled. After tonight her cheeks were probably going to be permanently stained pink.

As they continued down the hallway, Katie's eyes were drawn to the first room. She stopped as they neared the doorway. It had only been left partially open so she felt a little strange peeking in, but she just couldn't help it.

"What's the matter?" Seamus asked.

"I... I thought I saw something," she said as she peeked through the narrow gap.

"You probably did see something. But I thought you didn't care for the rooms that involved spanking."

"Yeah, I don't."

"So what are you doing?"

"Oh my God." Katie couldn't believe what she saw.

"What?" Seamus crowded in next to Katie, making all her nerve endings leap to life where they merged into each other.

"That's... That's Shanna!"

"Who?"

"Shanna." Katie turned to Seamus. "The lady with the ghost boyfriend. Remember, we saw them earlier in the lounge?"

Seamus stuck his ghostly head through the door. Katie couldn't decide if she should be jealous or glad she couldn't see as much as he.

"It is her," Seamus said. "And I think she likes that bench."

"God. Don't tell me." Katie backed away from the door.

"You don't want to know what they're doing?"

"I have an idea," she mumbled. "And I don't really want to keep it in my head. Especially if it's someone I kind of know."

Seamus stuck his head through the door again. "Hey..."

Katie groaned. "Now what?"

He pulled out of the door and looked at Katie. "Take a look," he said with a jerk of his head.

"I'd rather not, thank you."

"Really. You do." Seamus' serious tone caught her attention.

"Why?" she asked, drawing out the sound.

"I want to make sure I'm seeing what I think I'm seeing."

"Aaaww. What?" She moved closer to the door again, took a deep breath and looked. The image of Shanna locked on to the bench with her bare ass in the air was more than Katie needed to see. Seeing Shanna's boyfriend using the paddle on her made her even more uncomfortable.

Katie looked harder at Shanna's boyfriend. Not that it was hard to do. He was rather nice to look at. He was hard in all the right places. Especially there. Apparently he enjoyed their activities in the room.

Katie felt her face flame at seeing him in all his glory.

"I didn't mean for you to ogle him." Seamus sounded a little annoyed. "I just wanted you to see what he looked like now. And what he was able to do."

Was he jealous she had looked at another man? That was good, right?

"Look at what he's holding," Seamus hinted.

Katie switched her focus to Shanna's boyfriend's hand. He held a paddle.

"Wait a minute. How is he able to…" Not only could he hold the paddle, he used it on Shanna. *How was that possible?* Ghosts passed right through material items.

She turned to Seamus. His face was set in a stony mask. If he was half as shocked as she was that Shanna's boyfriend no longer appeared to be a ghost, his world had to be off-kilter.

"We need to go," Seamus told Katie.

"But—"

"Now."

Without another word, Katie followed Seamus out of the Dungeon and back to her room.

When they were safely inside, away from anyone who might be listening, Katie finally asked, "How is it possible that Shanna's boyfriend used to be a ghost but now he's not? It's not as if he can be suddenly undead." She hesitated then asked quietly, "Is it?"

Seamus paced near the windows, obviously agitated by what they'd seen. "No, it's not possible to suddenly be undead. But how is he suddenly not a ghost?" He sat on the bed next to Katie. "He died in the hotel. I remember the accident. And I remember how upset the Chichesters were." He looked at Katie. "But what did he do to regain his mortal body?"

"How about if I ask Riona? Maybe she'll have an explanation," Katie offered.

He nodded. "That's a good idea. I think I'll talk to a couple of the ghosts I do know. See if they know anything." He shrugged. "Who knows? Maybe he found a way to regain his body for a short time."

"Maybe." Katie's mind whirled with things she'd like to do if Seamus could regain his body. Even if it were only for a little while. "But I really don't want you to run off tonight."

"Why not? I'd like to find out if there is a way."

Katie reached for Seamus' arm but, as expected, her hand passed through. "After everything I saw in the Dungeon tonight, I really don't want you to leave me alone, Seamus. Please stay. At least until I fall asleep."

The heat and desire flickered to life in his eyes. It mirrored what was probably reflected in hers.

"I'm sorry. I'm so used to watching that I don't get as excited by it as I used to. I forgot it was all new for you." He leaned closer and slid his gaze down her neck to her breasts then up to her face again. "Did what you see excite you, Little Katie? Did it make you burn to be touched?"

Her lips parted and her eyes dilated. She nodded. "Yes. I want you to touch me, Seamus."

He got up and moved to stand in front of her at the end of the bed. He put his hands on her knees. The coolness of his spiritual body contrasted with the heat radiating from Katie's core. "Take your shirt off for me, love."

Katie toed her shoes off then reached for the hem of her sweater. She pulled it up over her head and let it drop on the bed beside her.

Seamus' eyes devoured her.

"That too." Seamus pointed to her bra.

Katie reached behind her back and unhooked her bra. She held his gaze as she pulled her arms out of the straps then dropped the garment on the bed with her sweater. Part of her wished she'd invested in sexier undies, but really, she doubted Seamus would notice them for long. He seemed far more interested in her being naked.

She watched as he reached forward and ran a hand over her breast. The nipple perked in response to the cold and the tingles from their merging. He cupped his hand around her whole breast, or tried to anyway. Then he brought his other hand up to cup her other breast.

Katie's mouth fell open and her breath sped up.

He flicked both thumbs over her nipples, making her tremble in response. Then he ran his hands down the sides of her chest, down her belly to the waistband of her jeans.

"Will you take those off as well?" Seamus pointed to the closure of her jeans.

Katie noticed his accent had become thicker. It did that whenever he became aroused.

She reached for the button and popped it loose then slowly eased the zipper down. Since he stood in front of her she couldn't get up to slide her jeans off, so she lay back on the bed. His eyes darkened and a muscle jumped in his cheek. She eased her jeans over her hips, pulled her knees up so she could slide the jeans the rest of the way off then dropped the jeans onto the floor beside the bed.

"God, what I wouldn't give to be able to run my hands all over your body," Seamus groaned.

"I can do it for you," she said quietly.

She didn't know where her bout of daring came from but decided not to question it.

"Do it," he commanded from his place at the foot of the bed.

Katie watched his face as she bent her arm and brought one hand up to her shoulder. He gaze stayed locked on her movements. She trailed her fingertips along her collarbone, down her breastbone to her bellybutton. Then reversed direction and moved back up to her breast. She stopped just as she reached the bottom curve and waited.

His eyes flicked from her hand to her face then back again.

Finally he raised his eyes to meet hers. "Go on."

She smiled. "Just making sure I have your attention."

"Believe me. You have my complete attention," he assured her.

A giggle slipped out before Katie could stop it. "Very well."

She moved to cup her breast then lightly stroked around and over the nipple. Drawing her other hand in, she slid it over her hip and over the top edge of her panties. Seamus' eyes were drawn to the motion.

After seeing so many erotic images in the Dungeon, she felt primed and bolder than usual. She slipped her fingers into her panties and teased the top of the narrow band of hair that covered her mound.

"Don't torment me, love. Let me see you touch yourself." He pointed to her pink- and-white panties. "Take those off as well."

Katie lifted her butt off the bed and pushed the narrow piece of cotton over her hips and down to her knees. She pulled her knees up and wiggled her legs until she had maneuvered her panties down to her ankles then dropped them off the end of the bed at

Seamus' feet.

His eyes tracked the fabric's fall to the floor then quickly returned to Katie's body.

A flash of embarrassment swept through Katie but she stamped it down. After all, she had just witnessed a dungeon full of people doing all sorts of kinky things. There was no reason she shouldn't please both herself and Seamus.

"You are so beautiful, Katie," he whispered.

His admiration shattered the last of her inhibitions. She ran her hands up her ribs to her breasts. She pushed them together and pinched the tips lightly. Then she moved one hand down her belly to her pussy.

Using one finger, she parted her folds and dipped it into her pussy to wet the end. She drew the moisture up to her clit and circled the nub, around and around. The combination of Seamus watching her closely and the physical stimulation ratcheted her need higher, making her squirm.

"I really wish you were the one doing this," Katie said quietly.

"So do I." His voice sounded hoarse.

"Of course, it'd only be fair if I were taking care of you too." She drew more of her juices up to her clit and increased her tempo. "Since I can't do it for you, will you make yourself come, Seamus?"

Surprise flashed across his face but he quickly masked it. Without further prompting, he unfastened his pants and let them slide down his thighs. Katie angled her body so she could see him better.

His beefy hand closed around his cock, preventing her from being able to see him in his full glory, but what she could see was just about right. It was a shame she couldn't see more of his delectable chest and body. It was an even bigger shame that she couldn't lick it all over.

"You better not take too long." Seamus drew her out of her reverie. "Seeing you spread out on that bed pushed me close to my limit before I ever started."

Katie let her eyes roam all over Seamus as she continued to work her clit. She used her free hand to play with her breasts. Pinching, pulling and stroking them. Adding more sensations to what she already felt.

Waves of pleasure built inside her. Her heels dug into the mattress and she fought to keep her eyes open so she could watch

Seamus.

"Almost..." she panted.

She bit her lip as she struggled to take that last step over the cliff.

Without warning, Seamus leaned forward and touched her pussy. The shock of the cold and the tingles from where their forms merged triggered her leap over the edge. She cried out and her legs shook from her effort.

Somewhere in the back of Katie's mind it registered that she had heard Seamus groan with his own release. The sound of their mutual heavy breathing was the next thing Katie became aware of. Rational thought, however, remained out of her reach for a bit.

Seamus lay down on the bed next to her. Somehow he'd managed to fasten his pants. She couldn't bring herself to even try just yet.

As she tried to catch her breath she asked, "So you really are able to, um..." She turned her head to look at Seamus.

He smirked. "I should think that would have been obvious."

She rolled onto her side to face him. "The most obvious sign is a sticky mess. But there isn't one so how does that works for a spirit?"

"I'm not sure, really." He linked his fingers behind his head and looked up at the ceiling. "When I come, I feel the same things I did before the curse. But when it squirts, it just disappears."

"Wow. That's kind of..." She searched her brain for an appropriate word. "Weird?"

Seamus chuckled. "Less messy though."

She grinned in return. "That's true."

14

KATIE woke earlier than usual with her head full of questions. Seeing it would be useless to try to fall asleep again, she rolled out of bed and dressed for the day.

Seamus probably wouldn't show up for another couple of hours. If she intended to talk to Etain, this would be her best chance.

She'd brought up the idea to Seamus of asking Etain about the curse, but he had shot it down immediately. He'd declared he would never go near Etain ever again and didn't want Katie around her either.

While she didn't blame him, Etain was probably their best chance for figuring out how to break the curse.

Katie made her way up the stone steps leading to the battlements. At least the steps were dry, despite it being another cloudy day. She couldn't imagine going up and down the narrow stairway during the winter. Or during an attack on the castle.

The conditions people had to live with five hundred years ago were mind-boggling. But if they never had regulated heating and cooling or indoor plumbing, they wouldn't miss them.

When Katie reached the top of the stairs she sat down to catch her breath. As she rested she scanned the area, looking for Etain's ghost.

Alastar, the spirit she talked to in the library, had assured her Etain could be found up here. Apparently Etain had been hanged directly below this part of the castle. Guests of the castle and other ghosts had reported seeing her pacing back and forth, particularly on stormy nights.

Katie was somewhat leery of confronting Etain. Her opinion of the woman had reached rock bottom for what she had done to Seamus, and Katie didn't know if she could hide her feelings. But she needed to ask Etain about the curse. It didn't help that Alastar said Etain tended to be irrational, if not violent.

At first glance the battlements appeared to be empty. Katie turned the corner cautiously.

The wind on top of the castle walls blew harder than below. Katie's hair whipped around her face, occasionally blocking her vision. From the corner of her eye she saw a figure floating near the shadows at the other end of the battlement.

She found a corner she could stand in, out of the wind, and watched the figure. The apparition was a woman with long dark hair, dressed in what looked like a crimson gown. She paced back and forth, muttering to herself. Katie couldn't hear what the woman said but she seemed agitated.

Uncertainty of the ghost's mental stability—if such a thing were possible—made Katie rethink her idea of approaching. Seamus would have a fit if he found out she had come up here. Even Alastar had tried to talk her out of it when he found out why she needed to know about Etain.

What harm could there be in talking to her? After all, she was a ghost. Etain couldn't do much to harm her.

With her courage screwed on, Katie left the safety of her corner and slowly made her way across the battlement. She had only gotten halfway there when the figure spotted her.

"Who are you? What do you want?" The figure took a step toward Katie. "This is my place. You don't belong here!"

"I'm very sorry to disturb you." Katie kept her voice low and gentle. The same tone she would use if she were speaking to a frightened child. "I wondered if you are the Lady Etain."

Some of the wildness left the figure's eyes. "I am. How did you know?"

"The gentleman in the library told me I might find you here."

"Why did you seek me out?" she demanded.

"I, uh… I wanted to meet you." Katie's mind raced to find a plausible answer. "I am… I'm apparently staying in what used to be your room." She added, "In the hotel."

"You must be very important to have been given such a fine room."

"Well, no, not really." When Etain's eyes narrowed in anger,

Katie quickly said, "I mean, I'm not, but my mother used to work here and she knew the owner. They were friends."

"Ah. I see."

The tension eased a bit when Katie saw her explanation had been deemed acceptable to the crazy apparition.

She continued cautiously. "I read a few things in the library about the history of the castle and wondered about your life. Would you mind talking to me about it?"

"A man came many years ago, asking questions too. I sent him away." Etain took a step closer to Katie, her ghostly hands balled into fists.

Katie immediately took a step back.

"Men are ignorant fools. They do not understand that which makes us do what we do." Etain placed her left fist over the place where her heart would have been then took another step closer. "But you. You should understand."

Katie forced herself to remain in place. "Um… Yeah. Okay."

Once again, some of the wildness left Etain's eyes. "Your manner of speech is unusual. You are not from Ireland?"

"No. I'm from America."

"I have heard of this place. People below," she waved to the courtyard and bailey below the battlements, "have spoken of it. It is a long way away, is it not?"

"Yes."

"And you are a guest here."

"Yes, that's correct," Katie said as she kept one eye on the exit. She hadn't realized craziness carried over into death and obviously Etain's mood could turn in a split second.

"What is it that you wish to know?"

Katie tried to think of the best way to ask about the curse put on Seamus, but suspected launching into that topic wouldn't get her anywhere. "You were married to a lord, correct?"

"I was."

"What was that like?"

A peaceful look passed across Etain's face. "In the beginning it was nice. I had lovely dresses and he gave me lots of jewels. He told me I was the most beautiful woman in the land." Her face fell as she remembered the past. "But the workers were always coming to ask for help or they needed him to settle some dispute. The late nights working in his solar became more frequent. Then he started traveling to check on the other estates. Leaving me here, alone."

She looked directly at Katie. Some of the wildness had returned to her eyes. "I didn't like to be left alone."

"Wives have complained about their husbands' jobs getting more attention for centuries." Seemed like a safe response and seemed to satisfy Etain's need to be heard, if not understood. "Long separations sometimes lead wives to look elsewhere for affection." Knowing she might be pushing it, she added, "Did you ever have someone fill that void for you?"

A dreamy look passed over Etain's face. "There were others," she said enigmatically then floated away from Katie. At least she acted embarrassed by having taken other lovers.

"Were any of them more special than the others?" Katie's pulse skipped and she resisted the impulse to hold her breath.

"One," Etain said quietly. Her face fell and her eyes strayed to the edge of the battlements. She floated to the short wall then stared off in the distance as if remembering something.

Katie asked quietly, "What was his name?" She needed to be sure who Etain referred to.

"His name was Seamus. He was a lowly woodworker but he was beautiful and strong. But he..." Her voice dropped and her shoulders slumped a little. "He didn't want me." Etain lifted her head. "I tried to get his attention by dressing prettily when he was around. I always wore my best jewels and made sure my hair was perfect. I ordered refreshments for him when he worked. I even tried to make him jealous with other men." She turned her head to look at Katie. "But nothing worked."

"What did you do then?" Katie urged her to tell more.

"One of my maids told me about a woman who sold love potions." Etain turned her gaze to the fields outside the castle walls. "I had heard of the woman before. She was a very powerful witch. So I went to her for help. I wanted something to make him fall in love with me." Etain faced Katie with wildness in her eyes once again. "But she refused to help me. Me!" Etain's chin lifted a notch. "The Lady of Tullamore."

"Why would she refuse you?" Katie asked.

"She said she couldn't force anyone's will. The potion she created would only enhance feelings that were already there. If he were attracted to me, it would make him desire me more. But if he didn't love me, it might make him hate me."

"So what did you do?"

"I took the potion." She smiled a wicked grin. "And her book of spells."

"Why?"

"So I could make my own potion," Etain snapped, as if she thought Katie should have known the answer already.

"But did you know how—"

"It wasn't difficult to do. The book had the ingredients and the way to prepare them. I just mixed a couple of spells together to make sure I got what I wanted."

Katie had to hold her anger in check. It took some effort to keep her voice level. "And did you get what you wanted?"

"No," Etain said flatly. "He vanished after I cast the spell. I don't know where he went."

"Really?"

"They tried to say that I killed him!"

"Did you not?" Katie asked, knowing she might be pushing her luck with Etain's stability.

"No! I... I just... The potion wasn't something that would poison him. I even asked the cook."

"So where did he go?"

"I. Don't. Know!" Etain's hands were fisted at her sides.

"Okay. Okay," Katie said gently, trying to placate Etain. "I hear you. Why don't you tell me about the spell you used?"

Etain collected herself after her outburst. "What I did was rather clever, actually."

The urge to choke Etain, even though she didn't have a throat or breath, rode Katie hard.

"In the spell book, right after the love potions, there was a spell for summoning someone to do what you wanted. I combined the two. That way, if he didn't love me when he took the love potion, I would still be able to summon him to me and make him love me."

"How do you make someone love you?"

"He just needed to see that I was the perfect woman for him." Etain became agitated once more. She paced along the walkway, seemingly talking to herself more than to Katie. "If he would have just made love to me, he would have known. It would have been clear that I could have made him happy. But no! He refused me, time and time again."

Etain stopped and looked at Katie. "He said it was because of my husband. That he couldn't betray his lord." She resumed her pacing. "But that didn't stop the others. I don't know why it mattered to him." She swung around. "I think he loved another woman and just didn't want to admit it."

Katie made sure she kept her face neutral and bit her tongue so she wouldn't say anything.

"But I got the last laugh," Etain said with a lift of her chin. "I made it so that he couldn't love anyone else but me. I made the spell so that I would be able to summon him until he gave in and made love to me. Once he figured out I was his one true love he'd declare it and the spell would be lifted."

Etain shrugged. "The spell book said the summoning spell worked on people who had died, but I thought it would work just as well on someone who still lived."

"It didn't occur to you that mixing the spells might do something else entirely? Like turn that person into a spirit?"

"Of course not. I don't believe in spirits."

The irony of the situation became too much for Katie. "Even now?" She had to ask.

"No," she said, as if Katie were a simpleton.

Katie's jaw hinged open in shock. The woman's shallowness astounded her.

"I still don't understand what happened the day they murdered me." She looked over the edge of the wall to the grounds below. "They set the gallows there, just below us." She looked up to the sky. "It was a dreary day. No rain. Just fog and mist."

She squared her shoulders and continued. "They came for me not long after the noon bells. I wanted Mary to go with me but they wouldn't let her. They wouldn't let her do my hair that morning either. Not even a simple braid.

"When I got to the platform, I begged them to let me go. I tried to tell them I hadn't killed anyone. That I wouldn't ever do that. But no one listened." She looked off in the distance. "There weren't many people there. And no one who cared about me. I was alone even then."

She touched her throat. "I remember how heavy the rope felt around my neck." She laughed. "Strange but that rope was lighter than most of my jewels."

Katie shivered in revulsion. "So how did you get here?"

"I don't know," she said with a quizzical look. "I remember

praying that God would come and take me away. Up to the clouds, away from everyone. I keep wondering if the angels dropped me on the way to heaven. So, I stay up here, waiting for them to come and get me."

The fact that she thought she should be in heaven pushed Katie to her limit.

"Well, I suppose I should get back downstairs." Katie forced a smile onto her face. "Thank you for talking with me."

Etain didn't acknowledge Katie had even spoken. Katie turned and headed to the stairs, thankful for the easy retreat.

15

AS Katie descended the stone steps she replayed everything Etain had said.

It was kind of sad how crazy Etain had become. Most of her issues were probably due to loneliness.

Before she reached the first landing, Katie heard a shriek from the battlements. She paused and listened. Suddenly a burst of air blew past, pushing her forward and against the stone wall the banister had been attached to. In the wake of the wind, Katie thought she heard a feminine voice that sounded a lot like Etain's. If Katie hadn't been gripping the banister, she probably would have tumbled down the stairs.

Luckily she simply turned her ankle a bit and broke the nail on her pinkie.

Katie righted herself and caught her breath. She tested her ankle then made her way down the remainder of the steps as quickly as she dared.

When she reached the bottom she returned to the main castle corridor through the doorway she had used to get out. She hadn't made it far when she heard a familiar voice behind her.

"Have you taken to exploring the castle on your own now?" Seamus asked.

"Good Lord, Seamus!" Katie brought her hand up to her throat. "You need a bell," she grumbled as she started down the hallway.

"What kind of trouble have you been getting into so early in the morning?"

She frowned. "I don't get into trouble."

"Then why are your trousers soiled at the knee?"

Katie stopped and looked down at her jeans. Sure enough she had a gray smudge next to her knee. Probably the same color as the stone on the stairway she'd climbed outside.

"I fell," she said then resumed her pace.

"What were you doing when you fell?" he pressed.

Katie tried again to minimize the incident. "The wind picked up while I walked down the stairs and I lost my footing. No big deal."

Seamus floated around in front of her and held up his hand to stop her. "The only stairs outside of the door you just came through lead up to the battlements." He crossed his arms over his chest and shot her a stern look. "You went up to see Etain, didn't you?"

Part of her brain recognized the danger in provoking Seamus while he was irritated but the other part didn't like being told what she could or couldn't do. "Yes, I did. I wanted to ask her a few questions."

Seamus' chest puffed. "I told you to stay away from her. She's too unstable and won't tell you anything helpful."

"That's not entirely true." She mirrored his stance and crossed her arms across her chest. "I found out more about the spells she used."

He paused, seemingly surprised by her comment. "It doesn't matter. You could have been hurt! I can't allow you to put yourself in danger trying to get answers to a riddle that may never be solved," he bellowed.

His concern softened her irritation. "Yeah, well, I didn't think the risk would be very big."

"It was." He pointed at her. "And I don't want you going near her again. There's no way of knowing what she might do to you."

"It went fine. Now calm down before you use up all your ghost-y energy. You still have to give me a tour."

He folded his arms across his chest again, but this time it was more of a sulk than a threat. "I'm not sure you deserve a tour today after going against my directive."

Katie wished she could kiss him on the nose. He was adorable when he was trying to be all alpha with her. "Remind me to tell you later about how much your directives turn me on."

A different kind of interest flickered to life in his eyes. "In my day, it was acceptable for men to take their women across their knee when they displeased them."

"Ooooh. And what if they liked it?" Katie teased. She'd never been spanked but knew some people got off on it. And her question served its purpose and completely distracted Seamus from being angry with her.

"Then they would have to find some other way to teach a lesson."

"Hmmmm." Heat flared between the two of them and Katie panties dampened. "So, what did you want to show me today?" She had to suppress the grin that hovered about her lips as they turned and made their way down the hallway.

She loved having her own personal tour guide of the castle, someone with firsthand knowledge of its history. But she was also thoroughly enjoying the other lessons Seamus had been giving her.

"What I'd like to show you would only lead to other activities, as you well know. So I thought I'd take you over to the Chichester wing."

"The Chichesters were the previous owners, right?"

"Correct. You saw the portrait of Lady Mary in the gallery."

Katie thought back to what she had seen in the portrait gallery earlier in the week. "Was she the woman in the wheelchair?"

"That's her. Sir Henry Chichester added a new wing to the castle back in the mid- 1800s to accommodate Mary's injury."

Seamus led Katie through a twist in the hallway. The small of her back tingled where he tried to physically guide her in the right direction. For the tenth time that week, she wished she could feel his touch.

"Henry was quite devoted to Mary and tried to make it as easy as possible for her to get around the castle."

"That's very sweet." Wouldn't it be lovely to be so loved by a husband? It was nice to know that not everyone married for titles or connections back then.

Seamus shrugged. "As you say."

Katie smiled.

They turned the corner that took them into the main lobby. She still became disconcerted whenever Seamus passed through part of a wall or furniture. How long would it take him to get used to being solid again and having to navigate around things once they broke the curse?

Surely they could find a way to reverse the spell. It just wasn't right for him to be forced to linger as a spirit because of some spiteful woman.

They made their way through the lobby without speaking. After touring half the castle with Seamus, it had become a habit for both of them.

Katie followed Seamus through the corridor of the newer part of the castle then into a passage she had not explored. When they were alone again, Katie asked, "So what happened with the Chichesters?"

"They both lived here until their deaths. Mary passed first. Henry didn't even last a year after she died. The family said they thought he couldn't bear to be without her."

"So it was a love match then? Not one of convenience?"

Seamus glanced in her direction, something unreadable in his eyes. "Apparently so," he answered slowly.

Unsure why that question would bother Seamus, Katie changed the course of her questioning. "Did Henry and Mary really pass over or do they still," she waved her hand in the air, "linger?"

"I have never encountered their spirits. But as you may have figured out, not all of the castle spirits choose to reveal themselves to me." In a quieter voice he added, "Nor do I visit this part of the castle much."

"Why not?"

He hesitated before answering. "I've heard stories through the years of unusual happenings in this part."

Katie's eyebrows shot up in surprise. "Unusual? What could possibly be unusual to a man who's had a curse placed on him and lives with ghosts, witches and God only knows what else?"

The look Seamus shot her was a combination of self-deprecation and irritation. Obviously he didn't like the fact that the stories bothered him.

"There has been more than one person who worked or stayed in this wing of the castle, never to be seen or heard from again."

The hair on the back of Katie's neck stood on end. "What do you mean? Like they just vanished?"

He nodded curtly. "That's exactly what I mean."

"Oh come on. People don't just disappear."

Seamus stopped walking suddenly and turned to face Katie. His expression was one of passive irony. If he had been solid, Katie would have plowed into him. She quickly backed up so she could shake the tingles she always felt whenever they merged, so to speak. Oddly the sensations she felt when she "touched" him seemed to be getting stronger.

Their eyes met and held. Heat blossomed between them again. Katie's nipples tightened beneath the layers of lace and cotton. It felt as if a thousand little pinpricks ran down the front of her body where he had passed through her. Not painful. It electrified her in a very erotic way.

"You feel that too, don't you?" Katie asked with a whisper.

He didn't respond at first, just held her gaze. The muscle in his jaw tensed before he replied. "Yes."

The raw need in his eyes sent a wave of desire coursing through her body. For the first time in her life, Katie knew what it felt like to be truly desired. To be desired fiercely and intensely. She knew without a doubt that if he could, Seamus would push her up against the wall and take her right there.

She shivered and tried to suppress the swamping need that threatened to overwhelm her. It would do neither of them any good to focus on the things they couldn't have. It would be better to focus on how to break the spell and take advantage of what few pleasures they could.

Seamus looked as if he had come to the same conclusion. When he stepped back, the level of intensity dimmed.

"We had probably best continue our tour," he suggested with a gravelly voice.

Katie cleared her throat. "Yes. Of course." With a forced smile, she added, "Lead on."

As they walked, they kept a little more distance between them in order to avoid any accidental brushes. She doubted either of them could stand a repeat of the near miss.

At the end of the hallway, Seamus led Katie into a sitting room Mary had frequented during her time in the castle. He pointed out a few of the unique collections about the room as well as some of the family photographs. The history accumulated within the castle walls fascinated her. By the time they left the sitting room, the sexual tension had returned to a manageable level.

Seamus led her farther down the corridor. "Since you liked Mary's sitting room so well, I thought I'd show you Sir Henry's study while we're here. Believe it or not, he had quite the collection of butterflies."

"Butterflies? Really?" Katie had trouble believing a hard-ass landowner would have a hobby that required such a delicate touch.

"Not many people knew about it."

"I should think not," she mumbled.

She tried to reconcile what she knew of the aristocracy of that time period and what she'd learned of Sir Henry when they passed an unusually wide doorway. For some reason Katie was drawn to it. She stopped walking and stared at the opening.

There were two wood panels that looked as if they slid into the left side of the doorway. The wood had been carved with a Victorian flair like many of the things she'd seen in this part of the castle. A metal grate at the top of the door appeared to act as a window, but was too high up for most people to look through. She could see another metal screen behind the window.

"Is this an old elevator?" Katie asked Seamus when he stopped to see what she was doing.

"It's a lift. Henry had it installed after Mary became confined to the wheelchair so she could access the upper floors without suffering the indignity of being carried."

"It's beautiful. Does it still work?"

"Yes, but only the family and a few of the braver staff use it now."

"Why? Is it unreliable?"

"You could say that," Seamus replied mysteriously.

"Could we use it? Would anyone mind?"

"There's nothing to say we can't." He shrugged. "I've heard people say they get a bad feeling when they get near it. Some have come right out and said they think it's haunted, so most people avoid it."

"Pish posh." Katie flicked her hand in the air to dismiss the idea. "Mother could see the future and I see ghosts, for Pete's sake. If it were haunted, I think I'd have the creeps, don't you?"

The doubt on Seamus' face indicated he didn't quite agree.

"Oh come on. Don't tell me you're afraid of a few ghost stories. You're a spirit, for crying out loud! What could possibly hurt you now?"

"It isn't me I'm worried about."

The soft, squishy feeling in Katie's chest came back.

Seamus stepped closer but kept enough distance to keep the tingles away. "You, Little Katie, are still mortal. I would be most displeased if something happened to you while I remained powerless to prevent it."

"It will be fine. Truly. I do not sense anything ill about it." She smiled up at him, reveling in the fact that he cared enough about her to worry. "I just want to ride up a couple of floors. I've never been in an old lift before."

He looked at the doors to the elevator as if they were a dragon that needed to be slain. Katie's palm itched to stroke the side of his face to soothe away his worries. Then again, she also longed to stroke his chest and, well, pretty much every part of him.

"Very well." He grimaced. "A quick ride to the attic can't hurt."

"Oh good!" Katie slid the wooden doors into the pocket of the doorway. "I'd have hated to leave you here while I rode it by myself." She tossed a teasing grin in his direction.

"You would have left me?" He sounded as if the idea were unthinkable.

"If I felt you were being unreasonable. Yes, I would have." She pushed the metal gate aside and stepped into the lift.

"Unreasonable," he grumbled. "When have I been unreasonable?"

The floor of the lift had been carpeted and, like the outer doors, the walls were wooden panels. For being almost a hundred years old, it was in remarkably good shape. An intricate design had been carved along the top edge of each wall that anyone with an appreciation for woodcraft would admire.

Sure enough, Seamus' gaze was drawn to it.

Katie inspected the metal panel near the gate. "So, which do you think? Three or four?"

"Three or four what?" he asked absently.

"Which floor should we go to?"

"Any of them should be fine for your purposes. You said you just wanted a quick ride, right?"

"Oh all right, party pooper." She pressed one of the buttons then waited.

"I believe you'll need to close the gate before it will move," Seamus suggested.

"Oh yeah." She looked at him sheepishly. "I'm used to elevator doors closing automatically."

After closing the gate, Katie returned to the metal panel. She pressed one of the numbered buttons again, only this time the box gave a little jump and the lights dimmed. Seamus instinctively stepped closer to Katie.

Above them the sound of a motor started then slowly the lift began to ascend.

"Isn't it wonderful?" Katie exclaimed in delight despite the creaks and groans the contraption made.

"Is what wonderful?" Seamus looked and sounded tense.

She held both her arms out, as if to take in everything around them. "The elevator or lift or whatever you call it. It's just grand!"

Seamus grinned back even though he seemed uncomfortable being in the small box. "It was quite the feat of ingenuity in its day. Many of the staff were fascinated when they learned what it did."

Katie clasped her hands together with a dreamy look in her eye. "I've only seen them in old movies but always thought they were rather romantic." She looked his way, one side of her lip curling into a grin. "When the bad guy wasn't chasing the heroine into one, that is."

"Of course," he said, even though Katie doubted he'd seen any of the old movies she referred to.

"One of my favorite—" The lift jerked to a stop cutting off what she wanted to say. The lights flickered. On reflex, she reached for Seamus.

Her hand connected with flesh and blood.

Katie's pulse pounded in her ears. Could she really feel Seamus? She feared moving away.

"Seamus?" Katie whispered. "Is that your hand I feel on my side?"

His hand inched upward. "You can feel this?"

She nodded slowly then looked up at him. "How is this possible?"

Without warning, Seamus' arms wrapped around her and he crushed Katie against his chest as his lips descended on hers in a long-denied kiss. He held her so tightly she could barely breathe, but she didn't care. She only knew she could finally feel him and that he held her and she didn't want him to let go.

Her hands moved everywhere. She wanted to feel every inch of him. She pushed his shirt up so she could could feel his back, chest and belly. When she brushed across one of his nipples, he jerked as if he'd been zapped by lightning.

Without taking his mouth off hers, Seamus backed Katie against the wall of the lift and trapped her body with his.

"I don't know how or why I can feel you," he rasped when he finally came up for air, "but I don't want to waste this chance." He attacked the closure of her pants with trembling fingers. "I'm sorry I cannot be gentle with you. I've needed you for far too long, Little Katie."

Katie's breath came in short gasps. "I don't need gentle. I just need you. Now." She wrapped one hand around his neck and pulled him back down so she could kiss him again.

When he failed to work the closure of her pants open, she pushed his hands aside and finished the job. As she slid her pants and underwear down over her hips, he loosened the buttons on his own but didn't let them drop.

Seamus dragged his lips away from Katie's and made his way down the side of her neck. Her breath caught when he found a particularly sensitive spot. He pulled her shirt and bra up and feasted on her breasts. She squirmed and gripped handfuls of his shirt as he teased each nipple with his tongue.

He dropped to his knees in front of Katie and pulled her pants and undies the rest of the way down her legs. She stepped out of one side but left the other pooled at her ankle in case the elevator started moving again.

He placed a kiss on the neatly trimmed thatch of hair at the junction of her thighs and breathed in deeply. Like a starving man, he pulled one of her legs over his shoulder and buried his face in her heat. The first stroke of his tongue against the most intimate part of her stole her breath.

He lapped and teased her sensitive bud and drove her closer to the edge. Despite being a spirit for over three hundred years, he still knew how to use his tongue. Finally she bowed against the wall as the fireworks went off inside her head. "Oh God, Seamus!"

Seamus lapped up her juices as she rode the wave of her orgasm then stood and pushed his pants down to his ankles. He picked Katie up then, using the wall as leverage, wrapped her legs around his waist and plunged into her still-quivering pussy.

With his forehead pressed against hers, he held still, giving her a moment to adjust to his invasion. The feeling of him finally being inside her was quite simply heaven. She pushed her hips against his, encouraging him to move.

He tried to still her movements by gripping her hips. "Have mercy, lass. I'm not going to last if you keep moving like that."

"Good!" she panted. "Move, please!"

"Ah, Katie," he muttered then crushed his lips onto hers.

It only took seconds for them to find their rhythm. Katie felt the familiar ripples in her pussy. She tensed and waited for the second wave to crash over her. When it hit, she clasped Seamus to her and screamed his name.

Her pleasure triggered Seamus' and they clung to each other as the world spun off its axis.

Slowly they floated back to reality. Katie could feel Seamus' heart pounding. She placed her hand over it and tried to memorize the sensation. As their breathing returned to normal, Katie noticed the tingles she usually felt whenever his spirit form passed through her body were coming back.

"No," Katie whispered. "Not yet. Please." She tried to grasp the front of his shirt but could barely hold on to the fabric.

Regret clouded his face. "I'm sorry, lass. I cannot control it. I would stop it if I could."

Seamus held up one hand. Katie guessed he could see the same thing she did. Her heart ached as more of the solid wall became evident behind him.

No longer supported by Seamus' body, Katie sank to the floor. Tears pooled in her eyes as she watched his corporeal form vanish once more.

Seamus squatted next to Katie and tried to reach for her, but his hand passed through her cheek. The familiar tingles followed. "I…" He started to say something but stopped. Nothing he could say would ease the pain and disappointment she felt.

The lights in the lift flickered.

"You had probably best get dressed, lass," he said softly. She nodded and slowly rearranged her clothing.

It was almost pointless since very few people could see him, but Seamus righted his clothing as well. As they dressed in silence, the lift began to move. When it came to a stop, Seamus looked in her direction.

Their eyes met and something unspoken passed between them. Both of them knew how lucky they were to have gotten even those few stolen moments together.

With one hand on the gate, she turned and looked back at him. "You said people had disappeared in the castle before and that it had something to do with the elevator." She hesitated. "Do you think we're still in the castle?"

Seamus shrugged one shoulder. "There is only one way to find out."

Katie nodded then pulled the lift gate aside. Before she opened the outer door, Seamus put his hand on hers. "Even if we're not still in the castle, we're together."

"Yes, we are." She smiled, took a deep breath then pressed down on the handle and pushed the door open.

16

"PERHAPS I should take a look first." Seamus stepped in front of Katie, cutting off her exit.

"Don't be ridiculous. I'm sure it's fine."

He crossed his arms over his chest and frowned.

"You just got through saying, 'there's only one way to find out', so let's find out."

Seamus refused to budge. Not that she couldn't have passed through him.

"How about if we look at the same time?" she suggested.

Seamus sighed and mumbled something about damn stubborn modern women but he did move to the side so they could both exit.

Katie stuck her head out of the elevator and looked in both directions. "We're right back where we started."

"Seems so," he agreed.

Oddly she was a little disappointed.

"Can I help you?" a young lady carrying a stack of towels stopped and asked. Katie guessed she was a hotel employee.

"No. We're...er, I mean, I'm fine. Thank you," Katie answered.

The young lady shot a wary glance at the elevator then bobbed her head and quickly proceeded down the hall.

Katie waited until the woman moved out of range then said, "I suppose we should head back to the room." She blushed. "I should probably take another shower."

Seamus scanned her from head to toe. The heat in his gaze made her squirm.

Wow, could she want him again so quickly? She had no doubt in her mind that if he were corporeal, she'd happily strip him naked as soon as they returned to the room. She had never been that way with any of her previous boyfriends. Why him?

"Might be a good idea," he said.

"So... What did you think of the old elevator?" she asked with forced cheeriness.

He looked at her with one raised eyebrow.

"I don't mean about that. Although I would kind of like to know what you thought of that also. But I meant about the actual elevator. I thought it had been remarkably well-preserved and functioned properly. Other than the whole..." She swirled her hand around in the air to reference their interlude.

The look he gave her said he thought she might be losing her mind.

"Don't you think the craftsmanship of the elevator was remarkable? The wood carvings. The polished metal. It must have been very well taken care of over the years."

"Most people are afraid of it. It is well-preserved because no one uses it."

"I don't see..." Katie's voice trailed off. She stopped and stared at Seamus.

"What?" he asked.

"You're doing it again. You're fading."

He held one hand up in front of his face. "Damn. I knew it was too much to hope for."

"Seamus." Katie's heart ached. "I don't want you to go." He might not be able to hold her, but she had grown to like his company and she didn't want to be alone right now.

"It will be fine. I always come back in the morning."

"Tomorrow morning is a way off. And what if you don't—"

"Don't borrow trouble," he cautioned her. "I will find you when I come back." He stepped closer and tried to touch her cheek but only left a patch of tingles.

As his form faded more, Katie told him, "Rest well."

"Stay out of trouble."

She watched as he vanished completely and sniffed back the tears that threatened to spill.

It took a moment but she shook herself out of her daze and headed to her room. She sat on the edge of her bed and toed her shoes off. Her mind wandered back to the interlude on the elevator with Seamus.

She could still smell him. Instead of ozone, she detected a rich, manly spice mixed with wood shavings. The thought of washing it off disheartened her but she couldn't skip taking a shower.

To delay a bit longer, she grabbed her cell and called Riona.

"Top of the morning, coz. How are you?"

"Fine. How are you?"

"Very well, thank you."

"What are you doing today?" Katie asked.

"Was thinking about making a run to the castle to drop off another batch of soaps later. What about you and your ghostly friend?"

"Seamus' batteries ran out, so he faded for a bit. I thought it might be a good day to for us to get together."

"For a little girl talk?" Katie could hear the smile in Riona's voice.

"Absolutely."

"That's an excellent notion. I have some information for you anyway. Shall we do tea then?"

Katie glanced at the clock. "What time?"

"About an hour? Down at the café?" Riona asked.

"Sounds good." An hour would give her enough time to take a shower and change. And maybe even pull herself together.

They finished their call and Katie headed to the bathroom.

An hour later Katie found Riona sitting at one of the tables in an out-of-the-way corner of the café.

"You look a bit flushed. Feeling a bit peaked?" Riona asked.

"I'm fine." At Riona's doubtful expression, she added, "Really."

Riona grunted. "I took the liberty of ordering a pot of tea and scones."

"Oh excellent. I didn't realize I was getting hungry until you said something."

"Good timing then." Riona smiled.

They exchanged pleasantries until the tea had been served. As they enjoyed their first cup, Katie told Riona, "I made a trip up to the battlements to see Etain."

Riona choked on her drink. "Alone?"

"Of course. Seamus wants nothing to do with Etain and refuses to talk to her. Besides, I'm not sure she would be able to see him."

"True." Riona put her cup down. "You appear to be unscathed, so I'll assume she didn't hurt you. What did she say?"

Katie shrugged. "She earned her crazy title honestly."

"Based on what I read in her journals, I agree."

"Oh that's right. You said you'd read them. What did you find out?"

"Nothing much. Her early entries were easy to follow. Lots of talk of dresses and jewelry and parties. By the end the entries had become whiny and more random. There was a lot of gibberish to sift through. The journals mostly confirmed that Etain wasn't trying to kill Seamus. She wanted him to fall in love with her and she didn't understand why he didn't."

Something twisted deep inside Katie's gut. Part of her pitied Etain but her more savage emotions burned hotter, making Katie wish really hateful things on her.

"My goodness, that's a hateful look," Riona pointed out.

"Yeah, well, Etain brings it out of me."

"And why is that, I wonder?" Riona took a sip of her tea and rolled her eyes away.

Katie thought she saw a smirk behind Riona's cup. "Oh whatever." She took a bite of scone.

"Your turn. What did you find out?"

"I did a little better than you. I got Etain to confirm that she did purchase a love spell but then she went back and stole the spell book so she could make her own spell."

"But what did she hope to make?"

"She said she was told the love spell would only enhance a lover's feelings. It couldn't make someone fall in love with her. So she decided to mix the love spell with a summoning spell. That way she could make him fall in love with her."

"Goddess above," Riona murmured. "She had no idea what she was doing."

"Etain certainly thought she did. She said it was easy."

"Harrumph." Riona slumped back in her chair with her arms folded across her chest and a frown on her face. It sounded as if she mumbled something about people meddling in things they knew nothing about.

"Okay, so we know what spells she used. And we know what Etain's intent was behind the spells. And we know how she delivered the potion. What else do we need to know to solve this?" Katie asked.

"There are a few more details about the potion that I would like to know."

"Like what?"

"Like, did she use fresh or dried herbs or extracts? And what kind of containers or utensils did she use? There are so many things that impact the effectiveness of a spell. I want to know as much as possible. Do you think Etain would talk to me too?"

Katie shrugged. "I don't know. It's possible but I strongly suspect it depends on the day and her mood."

"What did you tell her when you went up to see her?"

"I told her I had read about the history of the castle and was curious about her life."

"I bet we could play off that some more. Maybe tell her that we wanted to hear her side of the story."

"Would Etain know who you are?" Katie asked.

Riona shook her head. "I don't think so. I'm not aware that I've been around her, but it is possible. Even if she asked, I could just tell her that I'm helping you find more history of the area."

"True. When do you want to go?"

"I'm flexible. When did you go up to see her?"

"This morning."

"Oh. After Seamus faded out?"

"No. Before. He doesn't usually show up until midmorning so I made sure I woke bright and early so I would be done before he did."

"So he doesn't know?"

"Oh he knows all right. I ran into him as I came down from the battlements." She shrugged one shoulder. "He asked and I didn't see any point in lying."

Riona leaned closer to the table. "Did he flip out?"

"A little." Katie grinned at the memory. "I certainly heard all about why he thought she was too dangerous for me to be around."

"Hmmm." Riona had a look on her face that reminded Katie of her mother. "If you were just up there this morning, we should wait to see her again. From everything I read, she's too unpredictable."

"You're probably right."

"If we wait a day or two, how are you going to get away from Seamus or distract him?"

Katie tapped her cheekbone as she debated ideas. "I could tell him that we're going to do a girl spa day. Most guys run in the opposite direction when they hear that."

"True." Riona pointed at Katie with her teacup. "But we should do a spa day before you go back to the States."

"I'd like that," Katie said.

"Oh. I meant to tell you. I talked with Ma the other night. She's on her way home from Italy but it'll be the middle of next week before she gets here. She's dying to meet you and said you better not leave before she arrives."

Katie smiled. "Good. I'm glad she'll be here before I leave. I just hope she didn't change her travel plans because of me."

Riona waved her concern away. "Ever since I started running the family business, she has been running off with those friends of hers. Every couple of months she takes off for someplace new."

"That sounds wonderful."

"Have you done much traveling, then?"

"No. Not yet. I started working before I graduated college and have never stopped to take the time." Katie shrugged. "I have a list of places I'd like to see someday though."

"Your company doesn't give you vacation time?"

"They did. And unfortunately, now I have all the vacation time I could want."

Riona's expression conveyed her question.

"They sold the business and closed right before I came to Ireland."

"So you're out of work now?"

Katie nodded.

"Does that mean you don't have to go back to the States right away then?"

Katie blinked as the thought settled into her brain. "Well... I..."

"Because Ma and I would love to have you stay with us for a wee bit," Riona pushed, not giving Katie a chance to think about it overly much. "The cottage is small, but we'll manage. Ma would love to have the chance to catch up on your and Aunt Deirdre's life."

"I don't know. I mean, I suppose I could stay longer. The only thing I really need to get back for is Jenny. But, really, even that isn't a rush. And a little more time would help them."

"Help who?"

"Jenny. My best friend. She and I have been roommates since college but she recently got married so she and her husband are looking for a new place to live."

"Will you have to find a new place also?"

"No. Jenny and I are living in the house that Mother left me. It's a cozy little place on the south side of town. Just right for two people. But if Paul were to move in, we'd be bursting at the seams." Katie wrinkled her nose. "Besides, even though Paul is a great guy, I don't want to live with a pair of newlyweds."

"Don't blame you," Riona mumbled then finished her tea. "Well, think about it. We'd love to have you."

"I will think about it."

They ate in silence for a moment then Katie asked, "What about Etain?"

Riona got a distant look in her eye. Once more Katie was reminded of her mother. Whenever her mother took on that semi-blank expression, Katie felt certain she could "see" things in her mind's eye. Things that would come to be.

Someday she'd ask Riona more about her gifts.

"I think Thursday would be best." Riona smiled. "I assume you'll take care of distracting Seamus?"

The image of a very naked and sexually satisfied Seamus who was too tired to move flashed through Katie's mind. That would be one way of distracting him. Unfortunately the odds of getting him back into the elevator were slim. The story of the spa day would have to suffice. "I will."

17

A few days later, Katie and Riona climbed the stone stairs to the top of the castle wall.

"What did you tell Seamus that we were doing?" Riona asked.

"That we were doing a girly thing and going to the spa."

"It won't be a lie if we really do go to the spa after."

Katie turned her head and grinned. "Very true. Think we can get in?"

"I know the manager. I bet she'll work us in. Besides, this isn't one of their busier days."

"Excellent."

When they reached the top, they were both a little winded and Katie's thighs were screaming for mercy. They took a moment to catch their breaths and let their eyes adjust to the light before stepping out onto the battlement walkway.

"There she is." Katie pointed out the shadowy figure hovering near the wall. "Can you see her?"

"I think so." Riona squinted.

"Come on. Let's see if she'll talk to us."

They slowly made their way to where Etain floated. Unsure of their reception, Katie never took her eye off the figure.

Etain turned to face them as they neared her. "I remember you," Etain said to Katie. She tilted her head to one side. "Why do you seek me out again?"

"Lady Etain, we wondered if we might speak with you about something," Katie said, making sure her voice remained steady and calm.

Etain turned her gaze to Riona. "And who might you be?"

"My apologies, Lady Etain," Katie said. "This is my cousin

Riona. She has been helping me with some research."

Riona tipped her head to Etain.

Etain studied Riona. "You look familiar. Do you work down there?" Etain asked with a jerk of her chin in the direction of the main part of the castle.

"Occasionally," Riona said.

Etain's eyes narrowed.

"I sell soaps and lotions to the gift shop. Perhaps that is where you've seen me."

"Perhaps," Etain agreed then turned to Katie. "What is it that you want to know this time?"

"I have been reading through the history of the castle to learn more about its, um…" Katie scrambled for a word that wouldn't set Etain off. "Inhabitants. You see, my mother told me just before she died that she had met my father here at Tullamore. I hope to find out more about him through some of the books in the library. But yesterday I stumbled across something that made me think of you and what you told me."

"Oh?" Etain's lady-of-the-manor attitude grated on Katie's nerves but she forced her irritation aside.

"The book had a passage about a woman who had been found guilty of a murder. It also said that the body of the man she supposedly killed had never been found. The passage was dated around the time period I thought you were, um… Well, that you were accused." Katie patted herself on the back for being so diplomatic when she really wanted to rip Etain's hair out.

"I never killed anyone. Yet they treated me like the most horrendous criminal. My own husband didn't believe me!"

If Katie didn't already know Etain was crazy, she might be tempted to buy into her "I am a victim" act.

"We were thinking you should be given a chance to tell your side of the story. After all, the passage said nothing about a trial or witnesses," Riona stated. "Doesn't seem fair, does it?"

Etain's gaze became unfocused and her hands fisted at her sides. "No, it wasn't fair at all."

Katie instinctively stepped back, taking Riona with her.

"They called me a murderer." Etain floated toward them.

"But you didn't kill him, did you?" Katie forced herself to remain where she stood.

"No," Etain wailed. "I would never do that." She added in a

whisper, "I loved him."

Something twisted painfully in Katie's chest but once again she forced her emotions aside. She couldn't reveal her feeling for Seamus.

"Of course you did. You went to a lot of trouble to win him over, didn't you?" Katie suggested.

"I did," Etain said tearfully.

"But he didn't understand," Katie said simply.

Etain shook her head.

Riona stepped forward. "I understand the spells you used didn't work?"

The look Etain shot Riona was borderline hateful.

"Perhaps something was left out?" Riona suggested.

"I suppose it's possible." Etain sniffed. "The woman helping me was not experienced in that sort of thing. She might have failed to do something."

Katie mentally rolled her eyes. Of course Etain would blame someone else.

"I have studied the practices of local witches. Why don't you tell me what you did and maybe I can help you figure out what went wrong," Riona suggested.

Etain studied Riona. "I should have thought of this before." She stepped closer. "You know enough to do as you say?"

Riona shrugged. "I can't say for sure until you tell me the details."

"Very well." Etain gestured for them to follow her. She led them to her place next to the battlement wall.

"Katie said you used a love spell. Was it one you created or one you received from someone else?"

Etain looked down her nose at them. "I didn't need anyone to make it for me. I can read."

"So you made the love spell. You said something about a summoning spell too. Did I remember that right?" Katie asked, trying to deflect the tension that simmered between Riona and Etain.

"Did you use all of the herbs the spell called for to make the base?" Riona asked.

"Of course," Etain snapped.

"What about the moon phases and the time of day?" Riona pushed.

143

"Moon phases? What does that have to do with anything?" Etain asked. Her tone indicated she thought Riona to be a simpleton.

Katie put her hand on Riona's arm just as Riona drew a breath to respond. She hoped it would be enough of a reminder that she shouldn't rile the crazy woman because they needed information from her.

Riona cleared her throat. "Okay, so what about the herbs? Did you use fresh or dried?"

"Fresh." Etain frowned. "No, wait, dried." She rubbed her forehead. "A couple were dried. Most were fresh."

"Which ones?" Riona pushed.

"I don't know," Etain exclaimed. "Mary gathered the herbs for me. I just mixed them together. What does it matter?"

Riona took another cleansing breath. "Did you offer any blessings as you prepared your base?"

"Don't be silly," Etain said.

"What about words of power or chants when the mixture was delivered? Or immediately after?" Riona asked.

"I did not see the need for them." She added, "But I did try to tell my love what he needed to do whenever he woke up."

Katie had to swallow her revulsion as she imagined what Seamus must have gone through at Etain's hands.

"What did he need to do?" Riona prompted.

"I told you," Etain said to Katie then looked at both of them. "He had to tell me he loved me and then make love to me."

A growl rumbled in Katie's chest. Riona put her hand on Katie's back.

"That's it? Just make love to you?" Riona asked.

"But not just anywhere. He had to do it in front of his hearth," Etain said.

"Why his hearth?" Katie asked.

"Back then, the hearth was usually located at the center of the home. It provided heat and represented family and solidarity." Riona squinted at Etain. "You wanted more from him than just sex. You wanted his devotion and a commitment."

"But you were a married woman," Katie exclaimed. "You couldn't give that in return. Why would you demand it of him?"

Etain crossed her arms over her chest. "I didn't plan on staying married for much longer."

Katie and Riona both took a step back. "What?" Katie asked. "Did they do divorces back then?" she whispered to Riona.

Riona shook her head.

"I thought once he had fallen in love with me, we could run away." Etain looked out over the battlement wall. "Husband or no. We could be together."

Katie's mouth fell open. Riona's grip on her forearm was the only thing that kept her from calling Etain a delusional fool. Seamus wouldn't have run away with a married woman even if he had been stupid enough to fall in love with her.

"How did you plan on getting him back to his home where his hearth was?" Riona asked.

"That was why I added the summoning spell. So I could make him go where I wanted him to go and do what he was supposed to do." Etain always sounded as if she were talking to a simpleton.

"Was his home very far away?" Riona asked.

"It was," Etain said.

"It isn't anymore?" Katie asked, not really wanting to hear the answer.

"Of course not. We weren't going to need it so I had the mantel removed and the house burned."

Katie's breath seized in her chest.

"What did you do with the mantel?" Riona asked.

Etain narrowed her eyes at the two of them. Suspicion clouded her face. "I hid it."

Katie and Riona exchanged glances. Etain had become defensive. The odds of her revealing where she had hidden the mantel had dropped significantly. But it sounded as if they really did have a chance of breaking the curse.

Riona took a step forward. "I worry that the combination of the two spells is the problem."

"Why do you say that?" Etain was still leery.

"Based on what little I do know of these types of spells, some of the ingredients may counteract each other. Similar to the way an acid and an alkaline work together."

"A what?" Etain asked.

"An acid and an alkaline." Riona shrugged. "They are scientific terms."

"I know nothing of these things," Etain said haughtily.

"Sweet and salty," Katie offered.

Etain sniffed in disdain.

"Let me look into the ingredients commonly used in these types of spells and see if I'm right. We can come back and let you know what we've found out some other time."

Etain's gaze fell on each of them. "Very well," she finally said.

Riona pulled Katie by the elbow to the stairway. "Thank you for talking with us."

Katie was still too overwhelmed to say anything. She waved a quick farewell then both girls started their descent.

Remembering her last visit to the battlements, Katie whispered, "Better keep a grip on the banister."

"Why?" Riona whispered back.

"Trust me."

When they reached the bottom of the stairs, Katie breathed a sigh of relief.

"What was the banister comment all about?" Riona asked.

"Last time I came to visit Etain, she flew past me on the stairs and nearly knocked me down to the landing."

"She isn't stable," Riona said, shaking her head.

"No, she isn't," Katie agreed.

"Let's go in through that one." Riona pointed to a different door across the courtyard.

When they entered the castle, Katie could see they were not far from the dining hall.

"So what do you think we should—" Katie's question was cut off.

"What kind of trickery is this?" Etain's voice rose to a shrill pitch.

"Trickery? What—?" Katie turned and saw Seamus standing behind them. *Oh boy.*

"Katie, Riona, move away from her." The lethal calm of Seamus' voice brooked no argument.

Katie and Riona exchanged matching "oh shit" looks.

"How did you come to be here? They said you were dead!" Etain cried. "They killed me because of you!"

"I didn't die," Seamus answered. "Despite your efforts."

If he'd had physical teeth, Katie felt certain he would have been grinding them based on the way the muscle in his cheek flexed.

Etain turned to Katie and Riona. "You asked about the spells." She paused. "You're trying to help him break my spell, aren't you?"

She backed away from where they were standing in the hallway. "That's why you sought me out." She floated higher in the air and the crazed look Katie had seen on her face more than once returned. "It won't work! Only I can release him!"

She charged at Katie and Riona. Paintings flew off the walls as Etain passed. Tapestries rippled in the wind. A small table and all the decorative items that had been sitting on it crashed to the floor. It looked like a wild storm blowing about Etain.

"Run!" Seamus roared as he put himself directly in Etain's path.

"No, Seamus!" Katie screamed as Riona pulled her into the nearby dining hall then slammed the door behind them. "Wait! We have to help him." Katie struggled against Riona's grip.

"She can't do anything to him. But she can hurt us." Riona quickly scanned the room. "Under here." Riona pointed to the thick wooden dining table.

Riona pushed two chairs apart so they could crawl beneath.

Katie hesitated, fighting her need to go help Seamus, even though she knew Riona was right.

When something slammed into the doors with a loud thud, prompting Katie into action. She scurried under the table and pulled the chairs together.

Suddenly the doors to the dining room crashed open and debris and wreckage from the hallway blew in. The heavy chairs rocked back and forth. The movement started at the end closest to the doors and ran the length of the table.

The drapes hanging over the windows whipped wildly in the wind.

"Etain! Stop this tantrum immediately!" Seamus shouted.

"Tantrum? You think this is a tantrum? How dare you!" Etain yelled. "You know nothing about how I've suffered through these years!"

"You think not?" Seamus yelled back. "You think I enjoyed being made into a spirit?"

Someone really needed to kick Etain's selfish ass, Katie thought. But how do you kick a ghost's ass?

"Do something!" Katie said to Riona. "Like what?"

"I don't know! Don't you have a spell or a wand or something?"

Riona glared at Katie. "This isn't Hogwarts. I can't just whip out a wand and make things disappear."

"I know, but damn. We have to do something to stop that psycho."

A chair crashed against the wall next to where they hid.

"Alanna is not going to be happy," Riona observed.

"Yeah, but who is she going to take it out on? Us or her?" Katie indicated Etain with a flick of her thumb.

"She'll know who was responsible. Somehow she always knows."

"Get away from me!" Etain shrieked.

Katie and Riona stared at each other blankly. Was it worth the risk to look out from under the table to find out what was going on between Etain and Seamus?

"Do you think I enjoyed watching my family grieve over me, never knowing what had become of me? Do you think I enjoyed watching them die of old age and not being able to tell them goodbye? I couldn't even put flowers on my mother's grave," Seamus yelled.

Katie's heart ached.

"And why?" Seamus demanded. "Why did I end up doomed to this half existence?" Katie could well imagine the expression on Seamus' face. "Because I wouldn't give in to your selfish demands as so many others did? Because I didn't praise your beauty or worship at your feet?"

The wind and the debris died down.

"Why didn't you?" Etain asked in a whiny, almost childlike voice.

"Because I have never loved you and I never will," Seamus said calmly and without reservation.

Etain let out a shriek that was probably one decibel from shattering glass. It could be heard as she flew out of the dining room and down the hall. Hopefully she would go right back to the battlements and stay there.

Katie and Riona waited to see what would happen next.

"She's gone," Seamus said. "You two can come out."

Katie pushed the chair closest to her out of the way so they could crawl out from under the table. She rushed to where Seamus floated.

"Are you okay?" Katie studied Seamus from head to toe. Relief flooded her when he appeared to be unscathed.

"I'm—"

"What is going on in here?" Alanna demanded.

Riona dusted off her pants and looked to Katie. "I'll talk with Alanna. You make sure our avenging hero is okay."

Katie smiled her thanks and turned her attention back to Seamus.

"Are you really okay?" She reached out to touch Seamus but stopped herself.

"I am well. Etain did me no harm."

"I wasn't sure whether or not she could." Katie wrapped her arms around her middle. "I worried."

"I worried far more about you, Little Katie. Etain may be a spirit, but she has obviously figured out how to manipulate her energy over the years." He shook his head. "Given her tendency for drama, I'm surprised she didn't do more damage."

Katie looked around the room. "Looks as if she did plenty. I'm guessing the hall is not much better."

"I'm just thankful you're unharmed," Seamus admitted. "But it disturbs me that I could do nothing to protect you."

She automatically reached for him again. "You did enough. You faced her down and then distracted her long enough for Riona and me to get away and hide." Katie smiled reluctantly. "Riona had to practically drag me under the table and sit on me to make me stay. I couldn't stand the thought of you being hurt by the psycho ghost."

"Psycho ghost?" Seamus asked.

"Etain. She's crazy." Katie tapped her head. "Psycho. It's short for psychopath. Psychopaths are usually violent and have no remorse for people hurt by their actions."

"Ah." He nodded his agreement. "That is probably a fair description."

"Well, at least she's gone back to her favorite haunt," Katie pointed out.

"Yes and I don't want you seeking her out again," Seamus said sternly. "It's not safe. Especially now that she knows I'm not dead and that you and I know each other."

"Okay," Katie murmured.

"I mean it. I don't care about breaking the curse if it means putting you in danger. There is no… Oh. Did you say okay?"

"I said okay, Seamus," Katie said with a timid smile. His concern warmed her heart. If he worried that much for her safety it could only mean he cared for her.

"Good. As long as we understand each other."

Katie would have laughed at his deflated rant but knew he'd be offended.

The sound of Alanna clearing her throat made Katie turn around.

"Riona has explained the situation," Alanna said. "You have my sincere apologies for the trouble you have experienced here at Tullamore, Miss Ward. I have radioed my staff to see to the mess and ensure none of our other guests have been inconvenienced."

Voices and squeaky cleaning carts in the hallway caused all of them to turn and look.

"Ah, here they are now," Alanna said.

"I'd say someone was in a right state to do all of this," one of the housekeepers in the hallway said.

"Okay, enough gawking. Let's get this set to rights," the gray-headed matron in the group prompted.

There were murmurs of, "Yes, mum," and the crew descended upon the area.

"I believe Mrs. Thatcher has things in hand. Perhaps we could all retire to—" Alanna was cut off by one of the ladies Katie had seen working the front desk.

"Ms. Burke, you're needed on two. The fire alarm in suite 201 is going off."

Three pair of eyes swung in Katie's direction.

"That's my room," Katie said in disbelief.

"I'll be right there, Mary," Alanna told the woman. "Perhaps you should stay here, Miss Ward."

"Oh I don't think so!" Katie said as she shook off her shock.

All four of them ran for the lobby stairs, slowing through the main part of the lobby after Alanna mumbled something about not scaring the other guests.

When they reached the top of the stairs, she smelled burning wood and paint. As they drew closer she found smoke rolling out from under her door.

Katie started to slide her key through the lock but Alanna stopped her. "Let me check the door to make sure it's not too hot to be opened."

"Better yet, let me take a look and see what's on the other side," Seamus said then floated through the door.

The sounds of raised voices could be heard. Without looking, Katie knew the screeching voice belonged to Etain. What the hell was she doing in her room?

Without giving Alanna a chance to check the door, Katie zipped her card through the slot, but it wouldn't unlock.

She tried her key again. Still the light wouldn't turn green, indicating it had been unlocked.

"The lock may be overheating and not working properly," Alanna suggested.

Katie beat on the door with her fist. "Seamus!"

"Now you'll never be free of the spell!" Etain's voice carried through the door, along with the sound of her near-hysterical laughter. "Never!"

"Seamus! You don't need to be around her any more than I do!" Katie hit the door again. "Seamus!"

Suddenly Etain sailed through the doorway like a blur, knocking Katie to one side as she passed.

Seamus stuck his head back into the hallway. "You can open the door, but it's rather smoky in here. Better get something to put out the fire before it spreads much more."

"Seamus said it's okay to open the door, but we need something to put out the fire." She turned to Alanna. "Is there an extinguisher nearby?"

At that moment, as if wishing for them made them appear, a couple of hotel staff ran up, carrying extinguishers.

Alanna blocked Katie with one arm and gently ordered, "Please let us, Miss Ward." Alanna slid her key card through the lock, got a green light then opened the door and motioned the young men with extinguishers to precede her.

While they extinguished the fire, Alanna and Riona opened the windows to let the smoke out.

All the fire and damage had been centered on and around the fireplace.

"I understand that Etain is pissed at me, but why would she try to start a fire in the fireplace? Wouldn't it be more effective to torch the bed or something flammable?"

"Actually, ma'am, I don't believe it was started in the fireplace. It appears to me some of the wood was pulled loose on the trim then the fire was started," one of the young men pointed out.

Alanna, Katie, Seamus and Riona all moved closer to look.

"I believe he's right," Riona said.

"Hmmm," Alanna said thoughtfully.

"But why—" It suddenly occurred to Katie what Etain might have been doing. Her gaze flew to Seamus then to Riona. "She was trying to destroy the mantel."

"The what?" Riona looked at the destruction around the fireplace. "You're right," she exclaimed.

Katie looked at Seamus. His brows were furrowed as he watched the crowd of people in the room. She turned her back to Alanna and the hotel workers. "What did your hearth look like?" she asked Seamus as quietly as possible.

"I..." He shook his head as if he needed to clear it. "It was a simple thing. One of my first. Just a flat piece of wood." His hands were splayed in front of him as if he were seeing the mantel in his mind and running his hands across the top. "I carved a design that looked like plait work along the front edge." He finally looked at Katie. "I built it so I could add more later."

"We're looking for a simple mantel. It has some kind of plait work on the front," Katie told the group.

"Do you mean some kind of knot work carved into some wood?" asked the young man who stood closest to the fireplace. He was looking at the part that had the most damage.

"Uh." Katie looked to Seamus who nodded. "Yes, maybe."

"It looks as if there's another section or another, older mantel behind this one," the young man told them.

Katie turned to Alanna. "You said you were planning to remodel this room before long, right?"

"That's true," Alanna said cautiously.

"Since this is already badly damaged, would you mind very much if we pull this outer section away so we can see what's behind it?" Katie asked.

Alanna took a deep breath and surveyed the area. "Well. I don't suppose it will do any more damage than has already been done." Before Katie could let out a cheer, Alanna added, "But! I insist that a member of our staff be the one to do it." She raised a hand to stop any protest Katie was about to make. "I insist! You have nothing but your bare hands to pry that away. Let my people gather the necessary tools and return. I'm sure they will have that outer piece removed within the hour."

"Okay."

With a look, Alanna set the two young men in motion. "Would one of you please notify Callum that he is needed?"

"Yes, ma'am," they responded in unison as they headed to the door.

"Now." Alanna faced Katie. "I believe the next order of business is getting you moved to another room."

"But I—"

"Unfortunately I don't believe any other suites are available, but we can certainly find another room that will satisfy your needs."

"No, really, that won't be necessary."

"Of course it's necessary," Alanna said as if Katie were daft. "I can't have a guest sleeping in a room that is charred, smelling of smoke and potentially dangerous."

"If nothing else, you might want to move just so Etain doesn't know where to find you come bedtime," Riona pointed out.

Katie's eyes widened in alarm. Seamus mumbled something unpleasant under his breath.

"I hadn't thought of that," Katie muttered. "I believe a new room will be just the thing. Thank you."

Alanna nodded her approval. "I will take care of it immediately and return with new room keys."

"Oh here's the one for this room." Katie extended the key card to Alanna.

"Very good." Alanna took the card then breezed out.

"How about I help you pack?" Riona offered.

"Thank you. That would be great," Katie said, feeling a little weary after the events of the last couple of hours. She pulled her suitcase from the closet and set it on the bed, open.

Riona leaned closer and whispered to Katie, "What is he doing?" indicating Seamus with a tilt of her head.

Katie looked to where Seamus had squatted next to the fireplace. "I think he's trying to get a look at what's under there. Not that I blame him. It's probably his last hope for breaking the spell."

"God, I can't imagine living for hundreds of years thinking there was little hope for changing a situation that wasn't your doing," Riona murmured.

"I know. But if it turns out his mantel isn't under there, I don't know what he might do."

Katie's fears were mirrored in Riona's eyes.

18

BY the time Alanna returned with new room keys, Katie and Riona had most of Katie's clothes packed. Seamus had taken his place at the window and appeared to be in deep thought.

"I spoke with our handyman, Callum. He will be here shortly to look at the fireplace," Alanna told them.

"Okay, good. I think we've just about gotten everything packed," Katie said.

"Excellent. A porter will be up to take your things to your new room."

Katie knew it would be pointless to argue, even though she was perfectly capable of moving her own suitcase.

"I want to assure you, Miss Ward, that we will be taking steps to ensure a repeat of this situation does not occur," Alanna said.

Katie and Seamus exchanged a glance. How did Alanna think she'd be able to control a ghost? Particularly a ghost who wasn't quite sane.

Riona saw the exchange. "Don't worry. I'll ward your new room so Etain will not be able to enter."

"What about…" Katie waved in Seamus' direction to finish her question.

"I can create the wards so they only affect Etain. It's a little more difficult, but possible," Riona assured her.

Katie looked at Seamus with eyebrows raised in question. She wanted to make sure he would be comfortable with Riona casting spells around him.

"If it keeps you safe," he said with a nod.

She turned back to Riona. "Thank you. I'd appreciate it."

A rap on the door caught everyone's attention.

Alanna went to answer the knock. "That will be Callum." She stepped back to admit six feet of muscled, male perfection. He had dark hair that curled over his ears and along the back of his neck. The razor stubble along his chin and over his lip added a rugged, edgy look. His vivid, blue eyes were a sharp contrast to his deeply tanned skin.

Katie's jaw fell open and she stared.

"Callum, this is Miss Ward," Alanna said. Callum tilted his head in Katie's direction but didn't say anything.

"And you remember Riona," Alanna added.

"Riona," Callum said, rolling the R across his tongue. The way he said her name made Katie think Riona and Callum were more than passing acquaintances. Interesting.

Seamus floated over and stood beside Katie. When she looked up, he was frowning. Hard.

Katie mouthed to Seamus, "What?"

"You were staring," he said as he crossed his arms across his chest.

Katie smiled to herself. He was jealous.

Alanna directed Callum to the fireplace. "We need you to remove the mantel and the trim." Callum crouched next to the charred wood and looked at the damage. "If you can't take it off completely, we at least need you to pull it up or down or aside enough so we can look behind it."

"Does it need to be in one piece?" Callum asked, his voice a low rumble.

"I am not concerned with preserving this outer piece," Alanna said.

Callum looked at Alanna over his shoulder.

"We have reason to believe there is something hidden behind the mantel," Alanna explained. "So if you would use care with the wall or whatever else may be back there, we would appreciate it."

"Anything else I need to know?" Callum asked as he stood.

Alanna, Riona and Katie all exchanged looks. Katie shrugged. Riona shook her head.

"If we think of anything, we'll tell you," Alanna answered for the group.

Callum grunted in response then strode to the door. When he returned he carried a large bucket and a toolbox. He put both on the floor not far from the fireplace then pulled out a large hammer and a crowbar.

After surveying the fireplace and the damage once again, he went to work removing the decorative trim around the main part of the mantel.

All three ladies were mesmerized by the play of muscles in Callum's shoulders and back as he worked. His tightly fitted t-shirt allowed them to see every rippling muscle and his snug jeans hugged his ass as if they were made for him.

Katie leaned closer to Riona and whispered, "Do you think he'll be able to get that off without much trouble?"

Without taking her eyes off Callum, Riona whispered back, "Not that I don't want Seamus to find what he's looking for, but right now, I'm hoping it will take all night."

Katie's eyes shot to Seamus. His arms were folded across his chest and he kept throwing dark looks at Callum. Seamus looked less than pleased with their reaction to the handyman.

She would probably have to smooth his ruffled feathers later.

Truth be told, as lovely as Callum was to look at, he didn't make her blood heat the way Seamus could with a few words whispered in her ear. And every time she thought of their episode in the elevator, her body temperature rose at least five degrees. Most of the heat pooled between her legs.

"Well." Katie cleared her throat and the thoughts whirling around in her head. "I think I'll finish packing my things." She hurried to the bathroom to escape.

Without fail, Seamus followed her into the bathroom, wearing a scowl on his face.

"Not pleased with how things are going out there?" she asked, keeping her voice low.

"Don't know why they couldn't have gotten Ol' Pete to do that." Seamus flicked his thumb at the door.

"Perhaps Ol' Pete wasn't available?" Katie suggested.

"Harrumph," he said with a bit of a pout.

"You know, he's not as sexy as you," she admitted.

"He's flesh and blood."

"Highly overrated," she said with a smile.

"He has a pulse and body heat," Seamus countered.

"You give me tingles where we touch."

"He doesn't disappear into nothingness when he runs out of energy."

"Probably not, but he still has to rest. And eat." She tilted her head to one side. "He may sleep 'til noon and have the manners of a bulldog."

"I suppose that's possible," he said with the barest hint of a smile.

"Although, I have to admit..." she let her words trail off deliberately.

Seamus narrowed his eyes in warning.

"That Riona seems to have a thing for him."

"I figured she was just impressed with his oversized tools."

Katie burst into laughter then slapped her hand over her mouth to hold in the sound. "Oh stop it," Katie said between giggles. "You're just jealous."

"Damn right I am. I don't like that you were staring like a schoolgirl over that muscled-up workhorse."

Katie struggled to control her giggles. "I'm sorry. I probably was staring. I just didn't expect the handyman to be so," she waved in the direction of the suite, "well... To look like a cover model."

Seamus frowned.

"Based on the rest of the staff I've seen around here, I expected him to be a lumbering old guy with a gruff attitude."

"You just described Ol' Pete."

"Where did Callum come from then?" Katie asked.

"He's Pete's nephew, I believe. Been helping out ever since Pete hurt his knee late last year. This is the first I've seen of him though."

"Well, that's good for Pete."

"I think Callum has been having problems with some of the men around town though."

"Really?"

"He's not a local boy and some don't appreciate the attention he's been getting from the lasses."

"Imagine that," Katie muttered.

Seamus simply grunted.

"Tell you what. I'll put this last bit of stuff," she pointed to her makeup bag and the toiletries she had gathered while they were talking, "in my suitcase and we'll take it up to my new room. That way you don't have to worry about me drooling over stud- muffin out there." She smirked at Seamus to make sure he knew she wasn't serious about the drooling.

"That will give me a chance to have a few minutes alone with you."

She raised one eyebrow. "How did you plan to use those few minutes alone?"

"If I could, I'd take you over my knee for going to see Etain after I told you to stay away from her." With a pointed look he added, "Don't think I've forgotten that."

Katie smiled contritely. "We needed answers about the curse and she was the only one who could give them."

"She's crazy and dangerous!"

"I know," Katie said quietly. "I'm sorry I worried you, but can we please argue about this later?"

"Fine. Later. But I'm not forgetting about it."

"Okay." She sashayed to where Seamus perched on the bathtub ledge. "Can we also talk about that spanking later? Perhaps in a less punitive light though?" she asked in a low, sultry voice.

Just as she figured it would, the thought changed the expression on Seamus' face from worried to intrigued.

"Have an interest in trying that now, do ye?" he asked.

"Maybe." She added, "If it's with you."

"Ah, lass. If only I could."

"Let's talk more about that later too. After we find out what's behind that fireplace."

He pressed his lips together and nodded.

Katie could tell he was reluctant to hope. But she wasn't. She had enough hope for both of them.

She reached out and touched his cheek and let her love show in her eyes.

Seamus tried to hold her hand to his face.

Something passed between them. An unspoken promise. A sense of what might be.

"Come. Let's go see about your new room," he suggested.

"Okay."

She turned away reluctantly and grabbed her bottles of shampoo, conditioner and lotion off the counter. With one last meaningful glance at Seamus, she returned to the suite. Seamus followed behind.

Riona and Alanna were still watching Callum work on the fireplace. Neither spared them a glance.

Katie dropped her things into her open suitcase and flipped the lid closed.

"How's it going out here?" Katie asked Riona and Alanna. She could see a few small pieces of painted wood on the ground near Callum. The pieces looked like bits of decorative trim instead of the main part of the mantel.

"Fine," Riona answered.

"Very well," Alanna said at the same time as Riona. She glanced at her watch. "I'm pleased with the progress so far, but must return to my other duties."

"We don't want to keep you. I was about to take my suitcase up to my new room anyway," Katie said.

Katie got "the look" from Alanna once again. "Tug will be here to take your bags up momentarily."

She barely restrained the impulse to say "Yes, ma'am." Instead she settled for "Thank you."

"Your new room is in what we consider the new part of the castle. Tug can show you the way." Alanna turned to Riona and added, "When you have a moment, I'd like to talk with you about a little pest control. Please stop by my office."

Riona nodded once. "I'll be there shortly."

"I'll check in with you later." Alanna included each of them in her parting comment with her gaze, including Seamus, then swept out the door.

"Did you see that?" Katie asked in a whisper.

"See what?" Riona asked.

"No," Seamus said at the same time.

"I swear it looked as if Alanna could see him." Katie pointed at Seamus.

Riona pursed her lips. "Very possibly."

"Why didn't she say something?"

Riona shook her head. "Alanna is the height of propriety and caution. She would never admit to half of what happens at Tullamore." Then she added, "At least not to a guest."

"Well, I suppose that makes a certain amount of sense. Never know which guests might freak out," Katie said.

A tap on the door drew their attention.

"I'll get it," Katie offered. "It's probably the guy for my bags."

She opened the door and found the tall, thin, redheaded porter she had seen around the hotel a number of times during her stay.

"Ms. Burke said you have luggage that needs to be moved to a new room?" The porter phrased it as a question but really it came out as a statement.

"Yes. Come in, please." She held the door open and admitted the young man.

Callum looked up from where he worked. "Tug," he said by way of acknowledgement.

"Mr. O'Neil," Tug replied. He looked across the room and gaped when he saw Riona there. "Mistress Mac au Bhaird. I didn't know…"

For a moment the teen looked as if he might drop into a formal bow or faint. He regained control of himself and made a short bow with his head instead.

Katie and Seamus shared a mutual look of "What was that about?"

"Thank you for coming up to take care of my cousin, Tug. We appreciate it," Riona said.

"Your cousin?" Tug asked, glancing at Katie.

"She's visiting from America," Riona added.

"Ah." He glanced at the suitcase on the bed. "I understood everything was packed and ready to go?"

"Yes," Katie answered as she zipped the bag closed. "There's just the one suitcase. I can get my backpack and purse."

Tug picked the bag up and set it on the floor so he could roll it behind him. "I'll be happy to show you to your room. Ms. Burke said you had a key."

Katie pulled a card from her jeans pocket. "I do."

"If you'll follow me, then?" Tug suggested.

Katie turned to Riona. "I'll be back in a bit. I just want to check out the new room and put my things down. Are you going to stay here?" She cast a meaningful glance in Callum's direction. It boggled her mind how he managed to ignore everything around him as he worked.

"I think I'll pop down and see what Alanna needs while you do that."

Katie thought there might have been a blush staining Riona's cheeks and wondered at the cause of it.

"Okay. I'll see you in a bit," Katie said then stepped out into the hall. Seamus had followed Tug, who waited not far away. "Lead on, Tug," Katie told him.

"I hope you're enjoying your stay, ma'am," Tug said as they

headed to the elevator.

"Yes, thank you. It's been interesting, to say the least," Katie said with a smile for Seamus.

Seamus coughed. "Interesting? Not the word I would have chosen."

"Have you been to Ireland before?" Tug asked.

"No, actually I haven't."

Tug continued his line of questioning and supplied several historic facts about Tullamore on the way to her new room.

When they arrived, Tug asked for the door key. The formalities they observed were amusing. She handed over the key so he could unlock the door.

He held it open so she could precede him into the room.

She walked in and stopped in her tracks. Seamus didn't even notice and floated through part of her. She was so stunned by the room, she didn't even complain. "Oh my God. This looks like a honeymoon suite!" Katie exclaimed.

"I believe it has been used for honeymooners before," Tug said unhelpfully.

Katie stared at the oversized four-poster bed. It was a massive thing. Walnut or some kind of dark wood that had been intricately carved along the posts as well as the head and footboards. The linens were pale-blue and silver. From where Katie stood near the doorway, they looked like silk.

The entire room felt light and airy despite the dark, heavy furniture.

"I dreamed of a room like this," Katie mumbled, still stunned by everything she saw.

"I trust this meets with your expectations?" Tug asked.

"Uh, it's way more than anything I could have asked for," Katie said as she gawked at the room. "And if the bathroom is half as nice as the last one, I may just break down and hug Alanna."

Tug's eyes widened in alarm. He handed the door key back to Katie. "Here you are. If you need anything or find anything unsuitable about your room, please ring the front desk."

She shook herself out of her stunned trance. "I will. Thank you, Tug." She handed him a few bills as a tip. "I appreciate you bringing my things up and showing me how to get here."

"My pleasure, Miss Ward." Tug left and closed the door behind him.

"So." Katie turned to Seamus. "What do you think of the new room?"

"I think I want to see you naked, spread-eagle on the bed and tied to these posts so I can lick every inch of your body."

19

KATIE'S breath caught in her throat and a flash of warmth rushed through her body. She licked her lips.

Seamus tracked the movement of her tongue as he reached down and adjusted his crotch.

"Come here," he gestured with his forefinger.

She complied, readily but slowly. She felt a bit like a kitten circling a much larger cat.

As soon as she reached the place in front of him, he ran one finger down the side of her face, her neck and her left breast. Her answering shiver brought a smile to his lips.

He pointed to the bed. "Sit on the edge." Once she sat, he said, "Kick off your shoes and loosen your undergarment."

Katie held his gaze as she toed off her shoes then reached under her sweater to unfasten her bra.

"Push your top up so I can see those lovely breasts of yours." She did as he asked without saying a word. "Ah, there they are. Stiff and pink. They're just begging to be touched, aren't they?"

"Yes. They want to be touched by you, Seamus."

"Do it," he said gruffly. "Touch them for me."

Katie ran both her hands over her breasts. She pushed them in from the sides then ran the tips of her fingers over her nipples. They peaked even more.

She squirmed on the edge of the bed and bit her lower lip as she imagined Seamus' hands, or better yet his mouth, on them.

"God, I wish I could suck on those breasts."

"Touch them, Seamus. Make them tingle," she begged.

He stepped up to the bed and knelt in front of Katie. His eyes traveled slowly over each breast. Finally he laid his hand just above her pelvic bone. Their eyes met and he flicked his thumb downward across her jeans just above her clit.

A whimper escaped before Katie could stop it.

With his palm down and his fingers spread out, Seamus ran his other hand across her thigh, over her hip, across her belly then finally up and over her breast. The chill from his touch and the tingles where they merged sent a wave of goose bumps down her body.

He ran his thumb over her clit a couple more times, taunting her cruelly before pushing the other hand up her ribs, palm down. Katie arched her back, pushing her breasts farther into his ghostly palms. She wished like hell he could be solid.

"Seamus," she moaned.

"Touch yourself, Katie."

Katie squirmed on the bed. That wasn't what she wanted. She wanted Seamus. She wanted his touch. But that wasn't going to happen.

"Only if you do it too," she bargained.

The muscle in his jaw clenched and his nostrils flared as he inhaled.

He let his fingers trail over her body as he stood. With a quick tug, he opened the closure on his pants.

Katie shifted so she could peek at what he'd uncovered.

The sight of Seamus' beefy hand wrapped around his cock made her pussy clench in expectation. When he stroked himself, she had to fight the urge to lick her lips. Oh how she wanted to taste him.

Without taking her eyes off Seamus, she pushed her jeans and underwear off then touched her pussy. Her sensitive clit ached for relief.

"That's what I want to see." Seamus slid his hand down his cock to palm his ball sac.

Katie mimicked his movement by sliding her middle finger through her nether lips and inside her opening. As expected, it was more than wet.

With her finger coated, she drew the moisture up to her clit then traced small circles around the stiff nub. She couldn't stop her hips from jerking in response when she touched a particularly sensitive spot.

"Tell me what you're thinking about," he demanded. His voice sounded gruff.

"You." The lazy circles she had been drawing around and over her clit quickened.

"What am I doing in those thoughts?" His strokes became shorter and focused on the head of his cock.

"You're touching me." Katie's heartbeat sped up and her breathing became heavier.

"Where? Where am I touching you?"

"Here." Katie cupped a breast and rolled her nipple between her thumb and forefinger. "And here," she lifted her hips in blatant offering as she increased the pressure of her strokes on her clit.

"What would I do next?"

She struggled to focus on his face when her eyes were drawn to his hand. She wanted so badly to be the one to touch his cock.

"You would kiss me."

"Aye. That I would," he murmured.

Katie squirmed and tugged on the other nipple. She met his gaze but saw him in her mind's eye more than in reality.

"You would lean over me. There at the edge of the bed." She slipped her finger down to her opening and circled the rim. "And you would pull me to the end so you could bury your cock inside me," she said as she pushed her finger inside her pussy.

"God, yes, I would," Seamus rasped.

Katie's lips parted and her breath came faster as she stroked her clit with more pressure. "You fit just right. And it would feel so good as you rocked in and out."

She felt the familiar tension building and instinctively tried to rush toward the sensation. "Seamus, please tell me you're almost there," she panted.

"Aye. I'm with you, love."

A few more rubs with her finger sent her flying. Starbursts exploded behind her eyes. Seamus' groan of pleasure from somewhere at the foot of the bed registered with her but she missed seeing his last few strokes.

When she regained her ability to think, she lifted her head to find Seamus. He leaned against the bedpost with one hand with his head bowed. He seemed to be catching his breath.

"There you are," Katie said with a grin. "I hope you didn't use up all of your energy."

"Not quite. But it's a close thing." He straightened his posture.

"Oh dear." She sat up on the bed. "Please tell me before you just fade out." She looked at the clock on the bedside table then sighed. "We should get back to the other room. Riona will worry."

"You're probably right," he said as he re-buttoned his pants.

Katie rolled off the bed with a groan then picked up her clothes. It only took a moment to get dressed then she headed to the bathroom to clean up. Unfortunately she could do nothing about her unnaturally pink cheeks or the stupid grin plastered on her face.

It probably wouldn't hurt to brush a bit of powder on her nose though. She reached for her makeup bag but couldn't find it.

When she returned to the bedroom, Seamus asked, "Are you ready to rejoin the others?"

"Almost. I wanted to grab my makeup bag first." She pushed her suitcase over and unzipped it. She rummaged through her clothes, feeling along the edges. "Huh. I must have left it downstairs," she muttered.

"Do you mean the pink one from the bathroom?" Seamus asked as he leaned over her shoulder.

"Yes, that's the one."

"I don't remember you taking it off the counter."

"That's what I was afraid of," she grumbled. "I'll grab it while we're down there."

"You don't need any makeup anyway," he reassured her.

"Thank you." She smiled up at him. "I thought I'd try to make myself look a little less ravished though."

"But you're lovely when you've been ravished."

Her blush probably went all the way down to her toes.

Seamus, however, looked pretty smug as he floated beside Katie on the way back to her old room. Then again, it was impressive how many times he'd helped her come even though he didn't have a body. It had been more than any of her previous boyfriends.

When they reached Katie's old room, she had to knock to be let in since she had returned her keys to Alanna.

They heard creaking wood and a couple of raps of a hammer before Riona opened the door.

"There you are," Riona said as she stepped aside to let them pass. "I was beginning to think you'd gotten lost."

"No, we were just, uh, putting some of my things away," Katie mumbled, feeling her face get warm again.

Seamus failed to hide his smirk.

"Hmmm," Riona said with a speculative gleam to her eye. "Well, you're just in time. Callum has all of the smaller trim pieces off and he just started removing the main board."

"Can you tell if there's anything behind it yet?" Katie asked.

Riona shook her head. "He hasn't moved out of the way so I could look."

"That's okay. I'm just anxious," Katie said.

Callum dropped his hammer and chisel into the bucket with a loud thunk then grabbed a large pry bar. He looked at the piece of wood closely before wedging the pry bar into a small gap. He pushed against the bar but only got a small creak for his effort.

Katie and Riona held their breath as they watched.

Seamus' brow furrowed. He seemed torn between worry and excitement.

Callum moved the pry bar a bit, trying to wedge it into the gap a little farther. He gave another push, moved the bar a little more then pushed again.

Each time they heard a slight creak.

Seamus stood off to the side not far from Callum. The nervous energy rolling off him was palpable.

Katie asked softly, "Seamus, are you okay?"

He wiped one hand on his shirt and chuckled. "After more than three hundred years you'd think I would be over this urge to physically do something. I'd love to just rip that board off the wall."

"That's completely understandable," Riona said.

Katie nodded in agreement.

Seamus floated closer to Callum and tried peeking around his hands and tools.

Katie wished she could see how much progress Callum was making. From where she stood, it looked as if the gap had only widened by a fraction of an inch. Judging by the expression on Seamus' face, it wasn't nearly enough.

Callum stopped and turned to the girls. "Would one of you tell your friend here to move back? While the cold is nice after working up a sweat, I really don't want to have his ectoplasm or whatever he's made of now rubbing on me."

Katie blinked in surprise. How did Callum know he was there? Seamus' expression implied he was just as stunned as she. Riona, however, didn't seem to be at all.

"Seamus, would you mind?" Riona waved him away from Callum.

"My apologies," Seamus mumbled as he floated away.

Callum grunted then went back to work with the pry bar. Finally his push resulted in a long creak and a groan from the wood.

"Ri, would you grab a couple of those wedges?" Callum asked as he kept some weight against the pry bar.

Riona hurried to where Callum had pointed.

Katie and Seamus exchanged looks. "Ri?" Katie mouthed.

Seamus shrugged.

"Push those as far as you can into the gap on the top and bottom," Callum directed Riona.

Once she did and had stepped back, out of the way, Callum adjusted his pry bar and pushed against it once more.

They heard another satisfying groan and a creak then the wedges fell out of place onto the floor below. With a look from Callum, Riona picked the wedges up and pushed them into the gap again.

They repeated the motions a couple more times then Callum switched his efforts to the top edge. He worked that loose then focused on the bottom edge. Finally he returned to the place where he started. One more push on the pry bar popped the piece loose enough so Callum could grab it with his hands.

He dropped the pry bar into the bucket of tools and pulled on a pair of leather work gloves. Using nothing but brute strength, Callum pulled the mantelpiece away from the wall far enough to let them take a look behind.

Katie and Riona rushed in, crowding Callum and making him frown at them.

"Oh!" Katie exclaimed. "I think there is something in there. Callum, is that supposed to be there?"

"I can't tell if I can't see, now can I?" Callum said, deadpan.

Riona stuck her tongue out at him but moved out of his way. Katie followed suit.

Seamus hovered nearby and appeared hesitant to look.

Callum grabbed a flashlight from his bucket of tools and directed it behind the mantel he'd pulled loose. "Aye. There is an odd piece of wood right behind the main mantel. And it has some kind of carving on it." He waved the girls back when they tried to rush in again. "Let me finish pulling this other piece off first then we can all see."

Seamus paced near the windows but kept one eye on Callum's efforts. He looked so wound up, if he had a physical body, he probably could have ripped the board off with nothing but his hands.

Finally the outer mantel fell off and all three of them rushed to look.

"How odd," Riona said.

"Seamus?" Katie voiced her unspoken question.

There in the wall, covered in soot and dust, was a piece of wood. It ran the length of the outer mantel but the carved knotwork was clearly visible along the lower edge.

Seamus reached out to touch the design. When his fingers brushed the wood, he jerked them away.

"What happened?" Katie asked, concerned he had been hurt somehow.

"It felt like fire shooting through my finger when I touched it," Seamus explained.

"Did I just see someone right there?" Callum pointed to where Seamus stood.

Riona and Katie exchanged glances.

"I don't know. Did you?" Riona asked.

"Look. I know you two have been talking about or talking to someone I can't see." He crossed his arms over his chest. "I'm not a simpleton. I know there are things around here I cannot explain. And I know I saw something or someone right there," he pointed to the same spot again, "for a just second. Now, what the hell was it?"

Riona looked to Katie. Katie looked at Seamus.

Seamus shrugged. "You can tell him if you want. It won't bother me."

Katie gestured to Riona. "Go ahead. You probably know as much as me."

"You did see someone." Riona sighed. "His name is Seamus MacDonhnaill."

"Is he a ghost then?" Callum asked, his face serious and showing no sign of mockery.

"No." Riona looked to Katie for confirmation. "Someone put a spell on him a long time ago. But it went very wrong and turned him into some kind of spirit."

"So he isn't dead then," Callum asked.

"No." Riona shook her head.

"And does this," Callum pointed to the board he had exposed from behind the outer mantel, "have something to do with all of that?"

"We think so," Riona said.

Callum grunted. "What else do you need from me?" he finally asked.

"I, uh…" Riona hesitated and looked to Katie and Seamus.

"I don't know either." Katie turned to Seamus. "Is that your mantel?"

"It is," he said. "But now what?"

Hope blossomed in Katie's heart. Maybe they would be able to break the curse after all. "He felt a shock when he touched it. And Callum could see him for a second. Do you think it has something to do with the curse?"

"Maybe so." Riona's brows drew down into a frown. "Seamus, would you be willing to try again?"

"Don't suppose it can harm me overly much," Seamus said with a shrug.

"Please don't be a typical guy and keep touching it just because you think you can take it," Katie admonished. "If it hurts, let go."

He offered her a small smile. "You worry about me, yet don't think twice about seeking out a lunatic ghost, Little Katie?"

"Yes, well, what can I say?" she said with a defiant lift of her chin.

Seamus stepped closer and lowered his voice so only Katie could hear him. "I'd kiss you right now, if I could."

Butterflies fluttered in Katie's belly. "I wish you could."

"Okay, you two. Don't forget you have an audience," Riona admonished. "Sort of."

"Sorry," Katie mumbled. "So, what do you want him to do exactly?" she asked Riona.

"I'd like to know what happens if he makes full contact with the mantel. So if he can stand it, I want him to touch it with both hands. Callum, you're the only one who can't already see at least part of him now, so if you don't mind, can you watch and tell me what you see?"

"All right," Callum agreed.

"Both of you might want to stay back a wee bit," Riona said to Callum and Katie.

"What about you?" Callum said before Katie could ask.

"I can shield myself if I need to, but I can't protect all four of us," Riona told them.

Callum nodded but his lips were set in a firm line.

Katie chewed her lower lip.

Riona turned to Seamus. "If something goes bad, I'll do what I can to help you, Seamus. But since I don't know exactly what Etain did in her spell, I'll be guessing."

Seamus glanced at Katie. "Just make sure she isn't harmed and doesn't do anything foolish to try to help."

Riona gave him a small smile. "I'll try." She took a step back. "Give me a moment to cast a cleansing spell."

He nodded. "All right."

Riona closed her eyes and murmured something under her breath.

Katie felt a chilly breeze race across her arms and face as if someone had opened a window and let in fresh, cool air. She looked around the room to see if anyone else had noticed it.

Seamus' eyes widened and he glanced around the room as well.

Callum remained focused on Riona. For some reason the look on his face reminded Katie of an ancient warrior set for battle.

Riona took a deep breath and exhaled. "I'm ready." She opened her eyes. "Go ahead and try the mantel."

Seamus looked at Katie. In that moment she saw what could only be love shining in his eyes. Her heart leapt with joy.

Then he stepped up to the wall and grabbed the board. Without warning, it felt as if a storm had blown into the room. Seamus' hair stood on end and whirled around his face. The years of dust that had settled on the board scattered around the room. Katie heard some kind of chant or rhyme echoing in the wind but still Seamus held on.

"What's happening?" Katie yelled.

Then a second, shrill, female voice blew in. "Tell me, Seamus. Tell me that you love me and you can be free."

Etain. That crazy bitch.

"No," Seamus roared. "I've already told you I don't love you and never will."

Katie didn't think it possible, but the wind blew even faster through the room, forcing Katie to squeeze her eyes shut to protect them from flying debris.

"I know that you do, Seamus. You have to love me. It's the only way," Etain's voice called to him, obviously trying to seduce him.

"Seamus, let go of the mantel," Riona called out.

Seamus struggled with the board but he still held on to it. "I can't!"

Katie thought she heard shrill laughter, then more chanting through the howling wind. The wind picked up speed, making the dirt and debris feel like tiny pinpricks on her skin.

"Riona! Get Katie out of here," Seamus shouted. "Etain is here."

"No! I won't leave you, Seamus!" Katie yelled. She tried to crawl over to Seamus but Callum grabbed her wrist. When she tried to yank her hand away, he stopped her with a look then pointed to Riona.

Riona knelt behind Seamus in the center of the debris with her hands extended to either side. The expression on her face was of total calm. It was one she would expect to see on the face of a teacher working with a pupil. As if she were waiting for him to come up with the answer he needed.

Seamus fought to free himself from the board, but he couldn't. "Katie, you have to go! Riona, please, I'm begging you!"

"Why shouldn't she stay?" Riona asked over the rushing wind.

Seamus' jaw looked as if rocks would bounce off it. "I can't protect her like this. Get her out."

"Why?" Riona insisted.

Tears ran down Katie's face and she was torn between doing as Seamus asked and stomping over to the center of the windstorm and demanding Etain fix what she had caused.

"I don't want her to get hurt," Seamus yelled.

"Why not?" Riona continued to press.

"Because I love her, dammit!"

A shrill scream vibrated through the room. "No!"

Katie froze but her heart did loop-de-loops in her chest.

The wind stopped its wild, twirling motion, everything paused for a split second then the wind blew outward in one big rush, knocking everyone back onto the floor.

"What the hell," Callum exclaimed as he sat up, having landed on his ass about three feet from where he'd been standing. "Is everyone okay?"

"Oowww," Riona said, rubbing her head, as she rolled over onto her hands and knees. "I'm fine," she groaned. "Just a wee bit tender. Katie?"

"Here." Katie's voice and everything else shook. "What about Seamus?" She struggled to get up but winced and gripped her shoulder. "Riona, is Seamus okay? Can you see him?"

"Oh God," Riona whispered.

Katie struggled even harder to stand, still gripping her shoulder. "What? What's wrong?"

Riona knelt beside Seamus. He lay perfectly still. Riona reached out, hesitantly, to touch him. "Seamus?" she asked quietly.

Katie rushed over and knelt on Seamus' other side. Callum crouched next to Riona.

"Oh my God, Seamus. No!" Tears flowed freely down Katie's face. She grabbed his shoulder and pushed him onto his back with her uninjured arm. "Please wake up. Please wake up. Please!"

Riona looked at Callum, her face grim.

Katie wiped a few bits of dirt from Seamus' face. "You have to get up. Come on. For me, please."

Sill his eyes did not open.

"Please, Seamus. I love you. You can't leave me now." She dropped her face onto his chest and wept.

The rise and fall of his chest as Seamus inhaled deeply stopped Katie's sobbing. She raised her head and looked at Seamus' face. Then she looked to Riona with a questioning expression.

But Riona watched Seamus.

"He's real," Katie said as the thought finally penetrated her grief-stricken mind. "I can feel him." She splayed her hands on his chest and touched him everywhere. His chest, his chin, his arms, his face, his leg. Even her sore arm appeared not to bother her anymore.

"Seamus?" Katie called softly.

"Little Katie," Seamus finally murmured.

"Oh thank God," Katie said as she fell across his chest and hugged him.

Riona nudged Callum and pointed to the door. He nodded in agreement and helped Riona to her feet. The two of them slipped out, leaving the couple alone.

"I thought you were dead," Katie said between sniffles.

"I'm not sure I wasn't for a moment there," Seamus said as he pushed his fingers into her auburn tresses and rubbed the back of Katie's neck. He let his fingers trail through the length of her hair. "I knew it would feel like silk."

Katie lifted her head. "Are you okay?"

"A little weak, but I think I'm fine. Are you?"

"Very okay," Katie said with a watery smile.

"Good." He smiled then closed his eyes. "You did it. You broke the curse."

He opened his eyes. "With your help."

"And you love me," she said as tears pooled in her eyes again.

"I do."

"I'm glad."

He chuckled, making his chest vibrate. "Are you?"

"Umhmm." she nodded. "Because I love you too."

"Ah, my Little Katie." He pulled her higher up onto his chest. "I've been starving for your kiss ever since our ride in the lift."

"You may have one and then a whole lot more," she said as she leaned over and teased the edge of his lips with her tongue.

Seamus groaned and pulled her even more tightly against him. The feel of his lips on hers was a dream come true.

Katie deepened the kiss and struggled to get even closer. She inched her hips until she could throw one leg over his body and then straddled his hips. However, when she tried to raise herself up on her arms, she winced as she put weight on her injured shoulder.

"What's wrong?" Seamus asked.

"My shoulder hurts a little. I must have hit something when the spell went off or did whatever it did." She leaned over, keeping her weight on her good arm, and tried to kiss him again. "It'll be fine."

Seamus pulled Katie down next to him and turned so they were face-to-face on their sides. "You're not on your sore shoulder, are you?"

"No." She smiled and wrapped her arm around Seamus' chest. "Oooo. I like this. Thank you." Her fingers went to work touching every part of him they could reach.

He chuckled. "It is rather nice, isn't it?"

"So…" Katie said as she petted him. "Are you really okay? Does everything feel, er… Right?"

"Nothing hurts. I just feel like I could sleep for days." He nuzzled her ear. "But I want to make love to you more than anything."

"How about if I make love to you then?" She nibbled on his chin. "You just lie there and let me do all the work."

"Ah, my Little Katie. You are too good to me."

She traced the edge of his lower lip with her tongue then mumbled, "Oh just you wait." She kissed him slow and easy, the way she'd dreamed of doing for days.

His cock twitched against her belly in response. That part of him didn't seem tired at all.

Suddenly she stopped. "Hang on a second." Katie jumped up and ran to the bathroom and grabbed her lost makeup bag. Her haste made her fumble with the zipper. Thank God for Jenny and her overzealous attempts to find her a man. She grabbed one of the condoms Jenny had stuffed into her bag when she hadn't been looking and dropped the rest back onto the bathroom counter.

"What's wrong?" Seamus leaned on his elbow on the floor as she returned to the main part of the suite.

"Nothing's wrong, I just want to make sure we're a little more careful this time. Especially now that you're back to normal."

"Careful?"

She knelt beside him and held up the plastic-wrapped circle. "Don't suppose you became familiar with these while you were spying on everyone in the castle?"

"I didn't spy on everyone in the castle but yes, I did learn about condoms." He took the package from her and examined it. "As I recall, they stop the man's seed from taking root and keep people from spreading diseases?"

"That's right."

"I don't believe I caught any diseases before becoming a spirit, but I understand your desire to be, as you said, careful. And while I saw condoms used many times in the Dungeon," he handed the package back to her, "I believe I may need your assistance this time."

The twinkle in his eye made Katie think he wasn't completely serious about his request for help, but she didn't mind. "I would be happy to help you."

She laid the condom aside then slid her hand under his shirt and traced the planes of his stomach and chest. When she found a nipple, she ran the pad of her finger around the hardened bud. His breath caught when she pinched the sensitized peak.

Suddenly he flipped her onto her back and leaned over her. The look on his face made her wonder if he was about to devour her. What a delicious possibility.

"No matter how tired I feel, I cannot lie here and be a passive recipient. I've been aching for you for far too long, Little Katie."

She ran her hands up his back and pulled him closer. "Well, then, perhaps we can ravish each other."

"That sounds perfect." He closed the remaining distance between them and captured her lips. Their tongues teased and danced while their hands groped and desperately tried to remove all the barriers between them.

After struggling with the unfamiliar buckle on his pants, Katie pushed him back, breaking their kiss. They were both panting.

"What's wrong? Did I hurt your shoulder?" Seamus asked.

Katie quivered with need. "No," she quickly reassured him. "I can't undo your pants." She tugged at the waistband. "You need to do it."

He rolled to the side to work the closure. Katie took the opportunity to pull her shirt the rest of the way off then unhooked her bra and tossed it aside.

As soon as Seamus saw her bare breasts, his eyes darkened and he lowered his head to them. One of his hands gently cupped a breast as he slowly brushed his cheek across the other until his lips found her nipple.

He used her pebbled nipple to trace the outline of his lips, making Katie squirm in anticipation. When he sucked the tip into his mouth, Katie stopped breathing.

Seamus turned his attention to the other breast. She clutched at his back, trying to hold on to her sanity. The feel of the linen beneath her palms reminded her that he wore far too many clothes. She pulled his shirt up, trying to get to the man beneath.

"Off," she said, pushing the bunched-up fabric of his shirt as high as she could.

It only took Seamus seconds to toss the shirt away. As soon as their bare chests met, a ripple of electricity passed between them. They both stopped and their eyes met. She could tell he had felt the sensation, but neither cared enough at that moment to question what it might be.

Instinctively they reached for each other and fused their lips together. Katie's hands traced the muscles in his back and shoulder and she relished the feel of him lying across her. Her hands slid lower and found the edge of his pants. She hooked her thumbs into the waistband and pushed downward, trying to get them out of the way.

She wanted to feel him all over. And she especially wanted to feel him inside her.

Now.

Seamus must have sensed her urgency. He tried to unfasten her jeans but couldn't manage the zipper. He broke their kiss long enough to say, "Your turn." Then he tugged on one side of her unbuttoned waistband. "Before I rip them off."

A thrill shot down Katie's spine, knowing he wanted her as much as she did him. She smiled against his lips and reached down to work the zipper open. He helped her push her jeans down so she could pull her feet free of the offending garment. Then he quickly slipped out of his own pants.

The feel of his warm, solid body next to hers, nestled hip-to-hip, ratcheted her need even higher. She pulled one leg up and across the back of his knee. Meanwhile they hungrily devoured the other's lips and tried to touch every part of each other's body.

"Please, Seamus. Fuck me!"

"Not until you come first." He pinned her down with one hand on her chest as he scooted down her body. Then he pushed her legs open with his shoulder and free hand and buried his face in her pussy.

The shock of the invasion was too much.

"Oh!" She tried to arch her back but his hand held her firmly in place.

His tongue worked her clit into an immediate frenzy, sending her close to the brink in no time. When he ran his tongue down her nether lips into her opening, Katie tensed and stopped breathing. The licks back to her clit started her breath again. But the suction on her clit sent her flying off the edge, into oblivion.

Her pussy convulsed, seeking more, wanting what Seamus could give her. As she rode that wave of pleasure, Seamus placed the condom in her hand.

"Here, love. You can show me how to use this thing properly later." He helped her sit up. "Right now I need to be inside of you in the worst way."

She gathered her thoughts and focused on the package in her hand. With trembling fingers, she ripped the plastic open then rolled the thin membrane down the length of his cock. When she looked up at him, he was gritting his teeth.

"Is that all you need to do to it?"

Katie nodded.

"Good." He pushed her legs apart and pulled her to him. He barely had time to aim his cock at her opening before sinking into her body.

The feeling of him filling her set her blood on fire.

His first few strokes were long and leisurely, as if he too were savoring the feeling. "Ah, my Little Katie, I cannot wait any longer." He pulled her leg higher up and over his hip then slammed into her body.

Seamus' reaction and the friction from his rock-hard cock sliding in and out of her quivering pussy set off another orgasm before Katie had recovered from the first. She clung to him as stars danced behind her eyes and prayed she wasn't dreaming.

20

THE feel of their hearts banging against their chests was the first thing Katie became aware of when her brain starting working again. They were lying chest-to-chest, but Seamus must have been holding most of his weight off her. Instead of feeling squished, she was comfortable.

Even the hard floor beneath her back didn't bother her. She was in Seamus' arms and that was all that mattered.

He lifted his head. The tender look on his face made her wonder if he'd read her thoughts.

"My Little Katie. I never thought I'd be able to hold you like this."

Katie's eyes misted over. "I was a little afraid of that as well."

He looked up and then at their surroundings. "Bollocks. I'm sorry I took you on the floor like some rutting fool."

Katie grinned at him. "I'm not."

"I could have at least moved you up to the bed."

"Next time we can use the bed."

A grin spread across his face. "Aye. Next time." He buried his face in her neck and tickled her with kisses and razor stubble then lifted his head. "And the time after that." He tickled the other side of her neck. "And the time after that."

When he finished, Katie was squirming and giggling like a schoolgirl.

"But the time after that, we may have to move to the tub," he informed her.

"Fine by me."

"But first, I think we'll need a bit to eat. I find myself famished." He leered down at her breasts. "For more than just your delectable body, I'm afraid."

"Oh! Yes. We can do that. Oh my goodness!" She put one hand on each side of his face. "I imagine you are hungry. You haven't eaten in forever!" She planted a quick but smacking kiss on his lips then said, "We need to get you some food."

Katie shifted her weight and made him roll to one side so she could get up. "Lots and lots of food." Her excitement bubbled over.

"I didn't mean right away." Seamus lay on his side with his head propped on his hand, not making an effort to get up from the floor.

She kneeled beside him and traced a random pattern on his chest with the tip of her finger. "Oh, but I think we do need to get some food into you right away. You see, you introduced me to a dungeon full of possibilities earlier this week. So I made a list of things that I want to do with you." She leaned close, inches away from his lips and whispered, "You're going to need your strength to get through them all."

He chuckled then grabbed her around the waist and pulled her onto his chest. "Then let us find food quickly."

The kiss he gave her left Katie breathless and aching for more. His idea of staying on the floor sounded better with each second.

Finally they came up for air.

"How about we skip the restaurants and just call for room service?" Katie suggested.

"I had no intention of spending any of this evening in public. I do not wish to share you with anyone. Not even your cousin. I will be grateful tomorrow for her help in breaking the curse." He ran one hand down her still-bare chest. "And I mean to keep you naked all night long."

A thrill zipped down Katie's spine. "Let's go up to our new room and get away from all of this." She indicated the dust and debris around the room with a sweep of her hand. "I'll call Riona and let her know we'll be keeping a low profile tonight and will catch up tomorrow."

Seamus sat up but the effort seemed to tire him.

"Actually you should get Riona to meet us up there so she can ward the room," he suggested. "I don't want Etain coming around during the night."

"Good idea. I'll call her on her cell then we'll go up."

"First, what do you customarily do with these?" He pointed to his condom- wrapped cock.

"Oh. Yes. Sorry." She ran to the bathroom and grabbed a handful of tissue. When she returned, she told him, "Just pull it off and wrap it in these." She handed him the tissues. "Then put it in the garbage in the bathroom."

He tugged on the latex and grimaced. "I think I should do this in the bathroom."

Katie watched him cross the room and admired the play of muscles in his backside. Once he was out of sight she padded across the room to her purse and dug out her phone. As she waited for Riona to pick up the phone, she slipped her panties on.

"Hello?" Riona answered.

"Riona? It's Katie."

"Are you two okay? I've been wondering if Seamus felt all right."

Katie smiled at Riona's concern. "Yes. Seamus is still okay. He says he's tired but that everything feels fine. And he's hungry too."

"Oh good. That's very good."

"We were about to go up to the new room. Seamus needs to rest. I planned to order room service for him, but we were wondering if you would mind coming and warding the room first." Katie glanced at Seamus. He had pulled his pants back on but sat on a chair, trying to catch his breath. "We were worried that Etain would be in a tizzy and might try to drop in again."

"Oh she was in a tizzy all right."

"Uh-oh. What did she do?" Katie locked gazes with Seamus.

"She stormed through the lobby when she left the room. A few paintings were upset, some furniture moved around and a few breakables were tossed. More than one guest saw it and, needless to say, became a little disturbed."

"Oh my God. Was anyone hurt?"

Seamus tried to stand up from his chair but she waved him back down and crossed the room to stand next to him so he could hear what Riona was saying through the phone.

"Thankfully no, but Alanna is in quite a state." Riona lowered her voice. "She asked me to make sure that Etain could do no more damage to anyone or anything."

"You don't mean—"

"I'm afraid so."

"Oh my goodness." Katie looked at Seamus. His mouth was set in a firm line. "I'm sorry you got dragged into the middle of this. Do you need any help?"

Riona took a deep breath. "I may. I have Etain confined to one of the sitting rooms for now. The staff are keeping guests away. I was about to run home to consult a couple of the family journals before I complete the banishing spell." She sighed into the phone. "Needless to say, I haven't had to force a spirit to cross over. I've been taught and I'm sure I can do it, but I want to make sure it goes as it should."

"What can I do to help?"

"The energies would be easier to balance with three. Would you mind helping enforce the protection shield?"

"If it means sending Etain where she belongs, no, I don't mind helping. Who did you have in mind for your third?" Katie rubbed Seamus' arm. Based on the frown on his face, he didn't care for her agreeing to help.

"I have someone in mind, but I need to see if I can get a hold of them. Can I call you back in a few minutes?"

"Certainly. We'll go up to our new room and wait."

"Okay. I'll ring you once I have everything arranged."

Katie clicked her phone to disconnect the call then turned into Seamus' waiting arms. She slipped her hands around his waist and laid her head against his chest.

"Did you understand what Riona was saying?" Katie asked quietly.

Seamus inhaled deeply. His chin pushed against the top of Katie's head when he nodded. "I believe so."

"Are you okay with it?"

"It must be done. Etain was not happy in life and she only became worse after death. She would never have found the peace she needed to go into the ever after."

"You're probably right." Katie sighed, squeezed Seamus once more then looked up and smiled. "Come on. Let's get up to our new room."

Seamus kissed her tenderly. "Before I'm tempted to ravish you on the floor again?" He smiled.

"You can ravish me on the floor all you want. But I think we need to get you into bed and get some food into you before you fall over."

She kissed him once more then pulled away so she could find her clothes. Before she pulled her jeans on, she shook the dust off. The thought of wearing a bra didn't appeal to her at all, so she slipped her shirt on without it.

When she looked up, she found Seamus watching her.

"What?" she asked with a grin, unsure what to make of his expression. It was a cross between amusement and what she hoped was fondness.

"Nothing." He shrugged. "I just like watching you."

She moved to stand directly in front of him then reached to take his face in her hands. "As long as you like what you see."

He slipped one arm around her waist. "Oh that I most certainly do." He pulled her against him and kissed her. Katie's toes curled and she fought the urge to crawl onto his lap.

"We are never going to make it upstairs at this rate," she murmured against his lips.

"You're right." He kissed her once more then swatted her on the butt.

"Oh. I better get my makeup bag." She tossed a saucy look in his direction as she headed to the bathroom. "We'll need it later."

When she returned to the main part of the suite she found Seamus standing next to the fireplace looking at his old mantel. His brow was furrowed and he seemed undecided about something.

"What do you want to do about your mantel?" Katie asked.

"I'm not sure," he said slowly.

Katie threaded her fingers through his. "I'm sure they won't do anything in here until morning. And even then, I doubt Alanna would get rid of your mantel without talking to you first. Why don't you worry about it tomorrow? After you've rested."

He smiled down at her then lifted their linked hands to his lips. He placed a kiss on her knuckles. "You're right. Tomorrow."

21

KATIE and Seamus had just polished off the sandwiches they grabbed from the lobby café when Katie's phone rang.

"It's Riona," Katie told Seamus when she saw the phone number on the screen. "Good timing. We just finished eating," she said into the phone.

"Excellent. Can you meet me outside the sitting room in the east wing? Seamus should know where it is."

"Sure. Do I need to bring anything?"

"If you have anything you use for focus or protection, you might bring it. Otherwise, no."

"Okay. We'll be there in a few minutes." Katie clicked off her phone and turned to Seamus. "You still look pretty tired. Maybe you should stay here and rest."

He tossed his sandwich wrapper in the trash. "No." He held his hand out. "Let's go."

Katie smiled and took his hand. Together they went to the room Riona had told her to go to. They had to pass through a "this area being serviced" blockade and several staff members before they found Riona.

"Ah, good. There you are," Riona said in greeting. "Sure you're up to this?" she asked Katie, but glanced at Seamus.

"I think so. Just tell me what I need to do."

Riona gestured for them to follow. "Like I said earlier, I'll handle the actual banishment spell. I just need you to help balance the flow of energies and support the protection." Riona looked at Katie from over her shoulder as she led the way to the sitting room. "Did Aunt Deirdre teach you any protection charms?"

"Yes, but I'm sadly out of practice," Katie told her.

"You might be surprised how quickly it will come back to you," Riona said.

As they walked to the door, the hair on Katie's arms stood. She glanced around uneasily.

"You're probably sensing the wards I created earlier," Riona told her. "Most people could walk through them and at the most feel a slight chill or discomfort. You are a Mac au Bard so you are more sensitive to them."

"Does that mean I can't just walk through them?"

"These you could," Riona pointed to the sitting room door. "But it would always depend on who or what the ward was created to repel."

Katie looked back at Seamus to see how he was handling all the hocus-pocus. His lips were pressed into a firm line and his shoulders were rigid. Everything about his stance screamed discomfort.

She squeezed his fingers. He met her gaze and returned the squeeze.

"What did you bring for protection?" Riona asked Katie.

"Me," Seamus answered for her.

Riona startled at his answer. Katie gave him a warm smile and slipped her arm around his waist. "I also have mother's necklace." She held up the delicate gold cross suspended on the chain around her neck. It jangled against the pendant embedded with Katie's birthstone and initials.

"That will do nicely." Riona nodded. "I can tell you feel very strongly about the piece. It will aid you well."

"You mentioned a third to balance the energies. Who did you get?"

"That would be me," a deep voice said from behind them.

Katie, recognizing the voice, turned and found Callum standing behind them. His arms were folded across his chest and his normally somber expression was even more pronounced. He didn't seem any happier about their gathering than Seamus. Perhaps less so.

"Thank you so much for agreeing to help us. Again," Riona said smoothly.

"Here." Callum stepped past Katie and Seamus and handed an aged leather pouch to Riona. "It's ground sea salt. Thought it might be better than whatever you found in the kitchen cabinet," he told her gruffly.

Riona's mouth hinged open in surprise. "I... Why thank you, Callum."

"Don't mention it," he grumbled.

Katie shared a smile with Seamus. Her curiosity about Riona and Callum's history would have to be slated soon.

"Okay. Is everyone ready?" Riona asked.

The four of them looked at each other. Katie answered, "Looks like it."

"Since there are four of us I'd like for each of you take a position on the compass when we go in. I'll take the north, Katie, you take the south."

"Which wall is that?" Katie interrupted.

"It'll be the one on the far side of the room after you walk in." Riona told her. "Callum, you take the east."

He nodded once in agreement.

"And, Seamus, you take the west."

"Me? I know nothing of these practices," Seamus protested.

"You're a part of Etain's history and you're here. You might as well contribute to the circle." Riona said. "Don't worry. We'll tell you if you need to do anything."

Seamus looked to Katie. She was sure her worry showed on her face.

Once again he pressed his lips into a firm line but said nothing, just followed Riona into the room that held the psycho ghost.

Riona had said the small chamber they entered was some kind of sitting room. It had floral-patterned walls and furniture. The chairs were scattered around a few strategically placed tables where a butler might leave trays of tea and cookies. Katie could well imagine a handful of Victorian ladies chatting about the latest gossip from town in here.

In the center of the room, a silvery figure hovered below the room's ornate light fixture. Katie hoped the fixture was a gas replica and not the real thing. She wouldn't put it past Etain to set the room on fire.

"Slowly take your positions around the room," Riona said softly. "Make sure you're directly across from your opposite."

The four of them took their places, each keeping a wary eye on Etain.

Etain's attention remain fixed on Seamus. The eerie expression on her face kicked the butterflies in Katie's stomach into action. It alternated between childlike confusion and unadulterated hatred. Katie immediately regretted not insisting Seamus stay in their room.

Riona followed them, moving furniture out of the way as she entered making room to complete their circle. She made one more pass around the room, this time with the leather pouch in hand. Katie guessed she was casting her circle. As soon as she returned to her position at the north, she set the pouch aside and murmured a few words. Katie couldn't make out what Riona said, but the hair on her arms stood up on end.

"Etain Chichester, your actions have created discord at Tullamore and the owners have deemed your presence to be dangerous. They have asked that you move on to your rightful plane of existence."

"My rightful plane of existence? This is my rightful plane of existence!" Etain's chin lifted as she spoke and her hands clenched into fists at her sides. "I'm here, am I not?"

"Will you go willingly to take your place on the other side?" Riona continued as if Etain had not spoken.

"Where is it that you think I should go? This is my home. You cannot force me to leave." Etain looked down her nose at Riona.

"What keeps you here at Tullamore? Is there something you are tied to?" Riona asked.

Etain glanced at Seamus.

Katie shook her head. She knew Seamus felt only anger, scorn and resentment for Etain. It was sad how Etain twisted a feeling as beautiful as love into something ugly and virtually unrecognizable. Then again, what Etain felt for Seamus should never be labeled as love. Her actions seemed to be based more on the fact that she had been denied what she wanted rather than a deep, honest caring for another person.

"I don't know what you mean," Etain said.

"You are a spirit. Yet you remain on the mortal plane. Why?" Riona pressed.

"I…" Etain looked at Callum then Katie then back to Riona. "I don't know," she whispered in a childlike voice.

"Will you allow us to help you?" Riona asked.

"No… I…" She glanced about the room wildly, as if searching for something. "I don't need help. I believe I will return to the battlements now." Etain tried to float through the circle they created but was stopped by an unseen force. "What is happening? Why am I not permitted to leave?"

"We cannot let you return to the battlements," Riona told her softly.

"You have no right to keep me here!" Etain shrieked.

"On more than one occasion you have frightened guests who were staying at Tullamore," Riona said.

"I did no such thing," Etain protested. One of the small tables near Etain began to shake.

"The fire you set in one of the rooms today could have hurt many people," Riona continued. "If you have remained because of your part in the curse that affected Seamus, consider yourself unbound. The curse has been broken. It is time for you to move on."

"It cannot be." Etain looked stricken. "I was supposed to be the one to save him. Seamus was supposed to love me."

"I told you long ago I didn't love you," Seamus told Etain. "You putting a curse on me only proved that you didn't love me."

"But I do love you!" Etain wailed as she flung herself at the invisible barrier between her and Seamus. "And I know you could love me if you would only try."

Seamus shook his head. "After spending the last three hundred years in a half-life of your making, feeling anything more than contempt would be asking the impossible."

A second table near Etain began to vibrate, making the statues and books fall to the floor. "You are cold and unfeeling!" Other things within the circle close to Etain began to shake. Some of the smaller objects flew in Seamus' direction but were stopped by the invisible barrier.

Seamus ducked in reaction.

"Do not break the circle," Riona warned. She began to mumble something under her breath.

Katie felt a ripple of electricity in the room. She instinctively visualized a blue light surrounding herself as her mother had taught her to do. It was one of the most basic protection charms she knew.

Etain must have sensed the ripple of power as well because her attention shifted from Seamus to Riona.

"Seamus," Katie called out above the clattering of furniture and things, "I know you aren't familiar with this sort of thing, but can you humor me and do some visualization with me?"

"At this point, I'm willing to try most anything you think will help get us out of here," Seamus yelled back.

Katie smiled. "Imagine a bubble of blue light around your body. You need to be able to see through the light, but it should act as a shield to keep anything negative off you. Can you do that?"

"Sounds easy enough," he said as he kept an eye on what was transpiring between Riona and Etain.

Etain and Riona appeared to be locked in a battle of wills. Etain had created a whirlwind inside the circle. Debris and furniture were being tossed around and most of it seemed to be directed at Riona. Yet Riona didn't flinch or waver. She stood still with her arms outstretched and her lips continued to move. Katie assumed she was saying some kind of chant or protection spell.

Katie looked to Callum. His face was set in a grim expression as he too watched the pair of women square off. Katie could tell if he was given even a split second, he would pounce and take Etain down. How, she didn't know.

When a jagged-edged plate went hurtling directly at Riona before Katie could call out a warning, the plate shattered into dust. From the corner of her eye, Katie would have sworn she saw Callum make an unusual gesture with his hand at the plate just before it shattered.

Katie shook her head to clear it and returned her focus to reinforcing the protection shield. When she felt her own shield was complete she stretched it toward Seamus. She visualized her shield merging into his and enveloping them both.

"What just happened?" Seamus asked. "It was cold and windy but now it feels warmer and smells like you. Did you do something?"

"You know that bubble I told you to imagine?" At his nod, she continued. "I merged your bubble with mine."

"You can do that?" Seamus asked.

She couldn't tell if he was intrigued or alarmed by the possibility. "It's a basic protection shield. Mother taught me how to do them when I was little but I haven't done one in years." She laughed. "I guess it's kind of like riding a bike."

"A bike? I wouldn't know. I haven't ridden one," he said with a shrug.

Oh the things she would have to show him. She smiled to herself.

"I'm going to try to encircle Callum and Riona in the bubble also," Katie told Seamus.

"What do you want me to do?" he asked.

"Keep imagining the blue light around you but include me now as well." She smiled at him. "It helped me merge with yours when I focused on how much I love you."

"I can do that," he said matter-of-factly, which set her heart to fluttering.

Katie focused on extending her blue light around to Callum. As her push of energy edged closer to Callum, he yanked his attention away from Riona. He shot her a dark and menacing look until he realized her intent then reached out his hand and drew her energy closer. Making their connection no longer seemed like an effort on Katie's part. It felt more as though Callum pulled it toward him.

When it snapped into place, the two men exchanged a look across the circle then turned as one to Riona.

Katie continued to focus on the blue light surrounding them. She ignored the furniture and debris floating in front of her and concentrated on reaching Riona from both sides. She could feel the flow of energy expanding around the circle that contained Etain then finally it reached Riona.

Her head snapped up and she met Katie's gaze across the circle. Riona flicked both of her wrists upward and drew the band of energy to her. The connection snapped into place. Katie could feel the change in the flow around them. It was like a blending of flavors into something new, something stronger and yet still delicious.

Now that Katie and the men were maintaining the protection around them, Riona would be able focus her energy and efforts on sending Etain over.

With one last push, Riona recited the banishing spell. Etain froze in place, along with all the debris she had spun up around her. Etain's eyes widened and her spirit body began to fade out.

Seconds later, Etain disappeared and the debris fell to the floor.

Oh thank God. Katie sighed in relief.

"Is that it?" Seamus asked.

"She'll need to open the circle once she's sure it's safe so don't move yet," Callum answered.

Riona closed her eyes and murmured a few words under her breath. A light breeze brushed past Katie's face.

"Etain is gone," Riona reassured them. She walked around the circle in the opposite direction as when she created it and gave thanks to someone or something as she made her way around. When she had completed the loop, she looked to Katie. "Thank you for your help." She nodded to Callum then Seamus. "You two as well."

"Etain's really gone, then? For good?" Seamus asked.

"Yes. Her spirit has moved on to the next plane," Riona told him.

He nodded but didn't say anything. Katie went to stand next to him. She slipped her hand into his and squeezed. He returned the gesture and smiled down at her.

"So, I guess that means we don't have to worry about being interrupted later," Seamus whispered to Katie.

She grinned. "Unless it's room service."

"We don't have to answer the door for them."

"True." Katie's heart swelled with love. She could hardly believe they had broken Etain's curse. Seamus had been freed from that dreary existence and from Etain herself. She pushed aside all nagging thoughts of what tomorrow might bring and what she'd do if or when Seamus moved on to explore all that he hadn't been able to.

"I need to do one more thing then we'll get out of here and let the staff put the room to rights again." Riona interrupted Katie's rapidly deteriorating line of thought.

"What's that?" Katie asked.

"I need to cleanse the room and us," Riona said.

"How do you plan to do that?" Seamus' held a tone of wariness.

Callum stood nearby with his arms folded across his chest like a warrior who'd been told to stand down. Seamus' discomfort made his lips twitch into a half-grin.

"Relax. It's nothing invasive. I just need to burn some white sage. The smoke will dissipate any negative energies."

"That's it?" Seamus asked.

"That's it," Riona reassured him.

Katie patted him on the arm. "We'll get you comfortable with all this hocus-pocus before you know it."

"What I've seen you two do hasn't been bad but I could go the rest of my life without ever seeing Etain's brand of hocus-pocus again."

"Etain had no idea what she was doing," Katie reminded him.

"And even if she did, the intent behind her actions was purely selfish. She didn't care who she harmed or in what way as long as she got what she wanted." Riona shook her head. "That is not our way."

"Let's get this room cleansed. I've got a list of things to work on for Alanna before I can go home tonight," Callum groused.

"Of course." Riona rummaged through a bag that had been sitting on the floor near the door and pulled out a bundle of dried herbs and a lighter.

She lit the herbs and worked with it until it created a steady flow of smoke. Riona then walked around the room, wafting smoke around all the areas Etain had been. As she cleansed the area, she murmured some kind of blessing. Once the room had been cleansed, including all the dark corners, she circled each of them with the smoke.

When Riona finished she extinguished her bundle of herbs and set them aside.

"Is that it?" Katie asked.

"That's it," Riona said with a grin.

"Shall I open the windows?" Callum asked from across the room.

"Yes, please," Riona answered as she set about righting a few pieces of furniture. Callum had already picked a few pieces up and put them in place.

"Do you need us to help with anything else?" Katie asked.

"No. You two go ahead. I'm sure Seamus needs some rest," Riona told them. "Would you mind telling Mabel that she and her staff may come in now as you leave though?"

"Certainly." Katie waved to Callum. "It was good to see you again, Callum. But perhaps next time it can be under more normal circumstances?"

"Perhaps," he said cryptically.

The distant look in his eye reminded Katie of when her mother "saw" things. She wondered for the tenth time that day if he had his own gifts and, if he did, what they were. Maybe Riona would tell her later.

Meanwhile she needed to make sure Seamus fully recovered.

And she knew just how to do that.

She took his hand and pulled him to the door. "Come on. Let's go take full advantage of room service and that oversized bed."

"Sounds good to me," Seamus said with a twinkle in his eye.

22

STANDING at the top of the cliffs, looking out onto the ocean, Katie watched the timeless battle. The water surged and broke against the rock and sand time and time again, relentless in its assault. But the beaches and the rocky cliffs refused to relinquish their hold.

Despite the pounding of the surf, the area was peaceful. And beautiful.

Katie could see why her mother had loved it here.

She leaned back, silently asking Seamus to hold her. Without fail, his arms wrapped around her and he placed a kiss on top of her head.

Finally she turned around and whispered, "Okay. Let's go down."

He didn't need to say a word, just placed a gentle kiss on her lips. Katie smiled at him, thankful to have him with her.

Together they found the rocky path Riona had told her about. The one leading down to the beach below the cliffs.

Waves lapped at their bare feet as they walked along the water's edge, looking for a spot that felt right to Katie. She slowed then stopped along a patch of beach that lay almost in the shadow of the highest part of the cliff. They were far enough away that the water didn't rush upon the sand, but the area remained damp from the last high tide.

Katie looked at Seamus. "Here, I think."

He nodded then stepped to the side, upwind, giving her space.

"You don't have to stay if you're uncomfortable. I know Riona said it's not a spell, but I will understand if you don't want to be around when I do this," Katie said for the fifth or sixth time.

"I want to stay."

"Thank you," she said then focused her attention on the instructions and the blessing Riona had made her memorize.

Katie held the container with her mother's ashes in her hands.

"Blessings to the water before us." Katie turned and faced the cliffs. "Blessings to the land below our feet." She turned so she faced the water again then raised the container up to the sky. "Blessings to the sky above."

She positioned the container in front of her but away from her body then spoke the words Riona had given her.

> *A daughter thought lost*
> *Returns home at long last*
> *She found love at the wrong time*
> *But never erased it from her past*
> *What she couldn't have in life*
> *Let her find now amassed*

Katie opened the lid on the container then poured out the contents, letting the wind carry her mother's remains away. Once the container was empty she reached for Seamus' hand and watched as the cloud of ash floated in the air and down the beach.

Before the cloud disappeared from view, the wind changed direction and blew the ashes back in their direction. The cloud twisted and appeared to form a more defined line then headed to where they stood.

Seamus stepped in front of Katie as if to protect her. Instead of hitting them, the stream dipped to the ground and circled around then spiraled upward. It hovered above their heads for a moment then sifted to the ground in front of them.

As the ashes settled, they formed a new shape... The shape of a woman.

Katie gasped. "Mom?" she whispered.

"My Katie Bird," the figure said.

Seamus slipped his arm around Katie's waist, offering his silent support.

"Thank you for bringing me home again. I'm sorry your journey has been so difficult."

"Is it really you?" Katie reached her hand out to the smoky figure, unsure what to believe.

"Your homage to the elements and our connection to

Tullamore has allowed me a chance to talk with you. For just a moment."

Katie could barely see around the tears pooled in her eyes.

"I'm sorry I didn't tell you about your father," her mother's figure told her.

"I know why you didn't," Katie said.

"I believe had he known about you, he would have loved you as much as I did."

Katie nodded through her tears.

"I wish I could stay for the wedding," the figure said as it dissipated.

Seamus mumbled, "We haven't talked—"

Katie looked up at Seamus and smiled. "I do too, Mom."

The figure faded more. "I must go. Connor waits for me."

"Connor?" Seamus asked.

Katie and Seamus turned to look where the figure pointed. High on the cliffs they saw a man standing near the edge.

In her heart, Katie knew who he was, but when she turned to ask, her mother's figure faded away. On the wind, she heard her say, "Name the baby after your father, Seamus. He will be pleased."

As they watched, her mother's spirit appeared on the cliff. The couple embraced like lovers who had been apart for far too long. They shared a kiss then her mother looked down at them and waved. Finally the couple turned and walked away from the cliff, their arms wrapped around each other.

Katie knew when they climbed to the top of the cliffs, they wouldn't find anyone there.

"Are you all right?" Seamus asked.

"Yeah." Katie wiped the tears away and smiled. "So you got to meet Mom after all." She sniffed. "Sort of."

"Did she really say what I thought she said about my da?" he asked hesitantly.

"I'm afraid so." Katie watched Seamus' expression, trying to gauge what he might be feeling.

Seamus put his hand on her belly. "Do you think she's right?"

"Mom had a way of knowing things," she said quietly.

Katie saw Seamus' throat move as he swallowed hard. "I never thought—"

"Are you okay with the idea of a baby?" she asked. "I mean, if it turns out to be true. Because we don't know for sure or anything."

"Okay?" he asked. "I would be more than okay, Little Katie. I would be honored for you to be the mother of my child. Or children if we were so blessed as to have more."

Tears pooled in Katie's eyes again.

Seamus pulled her closer. "I would be doubly honored if you would marry me."

Katie thought her heart would explode with happiness but her mind cautioned her with two lingering doubts. "Are you sure you don't want to wait until we find out for sure? I mean about the baby?" She shrugged. "Besides, you've just returned to the land of the living, I'm sure you'll want to explore it a bit before you settle down with a wife and kid."

"I want to marry you, Little Katie, whether you are carrying my child or not." He took both her hands in his and pulled them up to his lips. He held her gaze as he kissed the backs. "I've waited more than three hundred years to find the woman I wanted to be with and I'm not about to let her go now."

The last of her doubts washed away with the tears that rolled down Katie's cheek. "Then yes. I will marry you."

Seamus crushed Katie against him and took possession of her lips. Just as he possessed her heart.

The End

If you enjoyed this book, please consider leaving a review!

ABOUT THE AUTHOR

Dena Garson is an award-winning author of contemporary, paranormal, fantasy, and sci-fi romance. She holds a BBA and a MBA in Business and works in the wacky world of quality and process improvement. Making up her own reality on paper is what keeps her sane.

She is the mother of two rowdy boys and two rambunctious cats (AKA the fuzzy jerks). When she isn't writing you can find her at her at the sewing machine or stringing beads. She is also a devoted Whovian and Dallas Cowboys fan.

Find Dena on the web at:

Website - http://www.denagarson.com/
Facebook- https://www.facebook.com/AuthorDenaGarson
Twitter - https://twitter.com/DenaGarson
Email – Dena@DenaGarson.com

OTHER BOOKS BY DENA GARSON

Paranormal/Fantasy/Sci-Fi Romance
Her Clockwork Heart
Mystic's Touch
Rege's Rescue
To London, With Love
Vordol's Vow
When Ash Remains
Who Wants Forever
Your Wild Heart

Contemporary Romance
Down to Business
Loss of Control
Risky Business
Snow Effect

Short Stories (Contemporary)
Cherie's Silk
Working It All Out

Find detailed information on all of Dena's books at:
http://www.denagarson.com/books.html

OTHER EMERALD ISLE
ENCHANTMENT BOOKS

Tell Me Your Secrets by Virginia Cavanaugh

Who Wants Forever by Dena Garson

Phantom Mischief by J.L. LaRose

Lord Griffin's Prize by Katalina Leon

An Irish Flirtation by Louisa Masters
An Irish Attraction by Louisa Masters

Crimson Lust by Rebecca Royce

Desire and the Djinn by Rea Thomas